Demetrios took a deep breath. "Yes, I have had mistresses."

He felt her tense under his hands and he held her harder, determined to make her listen. "But they have not lived with me. I have not woken up in the morning and shared breakfast with them in this house. I have never wanted that."

"And now you do?" Sam's voice shook and she hated herself for it, for wanting to believe him.

"Yes, now I do."

SANDRA MARTON is an author who used to tell stories to her dolls when she was a little girl. Today, readers around the world fall in love with her sexy, dynamic heroes and outspoken, independent heroines. Her books have topped bestseller lists and won many awards. Sandra loves dressing up for a night out with her husband as much she loves putting on her hiking boots for a walk in a south-western desert or a north-eastern forest. You can write to her at P.O. Box 295, Storrs, Connecticut, USA (please enclose a self-addressed envelope and postage for reply), or visit her Web site at www.sandramarton.com.

The Pregnant Mistress is the seventh book in her well-loved miniseries THE BARONS.

Books by Sandra Marton

HARLEQUIN PRESENTS®
2202—THE ALVARES BRIDE
2223—COLE CAMERON'S REVENGE

Don't miss any of our special offers. Write to us at the following address for information on our newest releases.

Harlequin Reader Service
U.S.: 3010 Walden Ave., P.O. Box 1325, Buffalo, NY 14269
Canadian: P.O. Box 609, Fort Erie, Ont. L2A 5X3

Sandra Marton

THE PREGNANT MISTRESS

THE BARONS

HARLEQUIN®

TORONTO • NEW YORK • LONDON
AMSTERDAM • PARIS • SYDNEY • HAMBURG
STOCKHOLM • ATHENS • TOKYO • MILAN • MADRID
PRAGUE • WARSAW • BUDAPEST • AUCKLAND

ISBN 0-373-12243-8

THE PREGNANT MISTRESS

First North American Publication 2002.

This edition published by arrangement with Harlequin Books S.A.

® and TM are trademarks of the publisher. Trademarks indicated with
® are registered in the United States Patent and Trademark Office, the
Canadian Trade Marks Office and in other countries.

Visit us at www.eHarlequin.com

Printed in U.S.A.

CHAPTER ONE

SAMANTHA BREWSTER was bone-weary even though she'd slept like a corpse the night before, but crossing too many time zones always did her in.

Why wait for a better moment to slip away?

The party was going full steam. Carin's and Rafe's guests crowded the living room; the band was playing a hot samba and everybody was having a blast. Surely nobody would notice if she left, not even her ever-diligent mother and sisters.

Sam took a sip of her *caparhinia,* savoring the sweet taste of the rum, and put the glass on one of the little tables scattered over the moonlit terrace. She'd done the right thing by making an obligatory appearance at the festivities. Now she could go upstairs, kick off her spiked heels, trade her green silk cropped top and trousers for a T-shirt and a pair of cotton panties and tumble into bed. That was all she wanted to do, after spending forty-plus hours waiting in terminals and getting on and off airplanes. Jakarta to Honolulu, Honolulu to San Francisco, San Francisco to New York because she'd wanted to make a quick stop in her apartment, and then New York to Sao Paulo...

Just thinking about it made her want to curl up right there on the flagstone terrace and sleep.

Sam grinned. She could just imagine her sisters' reactions if she did. And her mother's. Marta would be horrified, more horrified than she'd been a couple of hours ago when Sam had teased her about what she planned on wearing to Carin's and Rafe's party.

"Jeans and a T-shirt?" Marta had said, staring at Sam as if she were a changeling who'd been dumped on the doorstep at birth. "To your sister's fifth anniversary party? Honestly, Samantha…"

"Honestly, Mom, Sam's kidding." Carin had shot a beseeching look at her over their mother's head. "Isn't that right, Sam? You're just joking."

"Of course she is," Amanda had said quickly, flashing the same 'oh please, don't make a scene' look.

Too bad, Sam thought ruefully. Marriage changed people. Once upon a time, her sisters would have known a gag when they heard it. Of course, she'd been joking. Even she knew better than to turn up at a party like this in jeans. It was just that she was tired to start with and when she realized her ever-hopeful family was still trying to get her Settled Down and Married, well, she'd gone from tired to cranky in the blink of an eye.

So, okay. Sam ran her hands through her hair even though she knew it wouldn't do much good. The humid Brazilian night had turned the tumbling auburn waves into a mass of wild curls despite enough hair spray to lacquer the entire chorus line in a Las Vegas production but she supposed she looked civilized enough to go back through the living room, nodding and smiling to anybody foolish enough to try and engage her in conversation. She could probably even assure Carin she was having a wonderful time, if she bumped into her. All she had to do was make it through the hall, to the stairs, and…

Sam's breath caught.

A man had just entered the living room. He was tall, with the kind of wide-shouldered, lean-hipped, long-legged body that did justice to his black tux. His hair was the color of midnight, his eyes were blue or gray—it was hard to tell, at this distance—and were set in a face that was all hard lines and chiseled bones.

He was, to put it bluntly, a gorgeous specimen. A woman would have to be dead not to notice. Suddenly Sam didn't feel quite so tired anymore.

If her sisters wanted to play matchmaker, why didn't they

set her up with someone like this? Not that it would get them the desired result. Handsome or not—and on a scale from one to ten, this guy was an absolute twelve—she wasn't interested in settling down…and that, Sam thought with a sigh, was the reason her family never steered her to hunks.

Men who looked like this weren't Suitable. They didn't have Marriage on their minds any more than she did. She'd heard the speech often in the days when she'd still been foolish enough to take the latest man in her life to some family function.

"He's charming," Marta would say during the inevitable post-mortem, "and handsome, of course. But, darling, you know he's not husband material. He's, well, he's Unsuitable."

Well, yes. Unsuitable for marriage, maybe, but marriage wasn't the only reason a woman would want a man. And Sam would tell her mother she was right, that Jason or Brad or Charlie was definitely not a man who would ever Marry and Settle Down and that was fine because she wasn't a woman who was interested in those things, either.

Unfortunately, her mother just wouldn't believe it. Neither would her sisters, now that they were married. Sam had become her sisters' Project. They'd taken up their mother's cause. That was why she knew, in her bones, that somewhere in this crowd lurked the newest in the long list of men who were Eminently Suitable, someone her family was convinced she would just adore.

Mister Eminently Suitable. Mister Deadly Dull.

Sam took her glass from the table and sipped at her drink. The hell she would.

She wouldn't adore any man with marriage on his mind, who'd want to clip her wings, put her into a gilded cage, turn her from a world-class translator fluent in half a dozen languages into a kitchen-class housefrau with a hundred recipes at her fingertips.

Her family actually thought that would make her happy.

It was the reason they kept introducing her to the Eminently Suitable men they believed capable of transforming and reforming her. Last time, Marta had come up with a stodgy academic twenty years her senior. The time before that, it had been a widowed rancher who'd given her a fascinating evening telling her all about the finer points of bull semen.

The truth was that both men had been nice enough, but Sam wasn't looking for nice. She was looking for freedom, adventure, and an occasional liaison with the kind of man who could make her blood heat without even touching her.

Someone like the Twelve who'd strolled through the door a few minutes ago.

Sam scanned the room. Where was he? Ah. There he was, talking with a blonde who looked as if she'd be happy if he'd strip her naked right then and there. No. Her sisters wouldn't introduce her to anyone like him. Since their marriages, they seemed to think they were the only Brewster women who could safely be involved with dangerously sexy types.

"The kinds of men you date won't ever settle down," Amanda had said primly at breakfast, and Sam had thought, sadly, *Mandy, Mandy, what happened to you?* Was her sister turning into a Marta-clone?

"That's right," Sam had replied, just as seriously. "That's what makes them so much more interesting."

Carin had sighed, and Amanda had sighed, and the only thing that had saved them all was that Sam had sighed, too, with all the drama she could muster. Her sisters had tried to look stern but, thank goodness, they hadn't been able to pull it off. All three of them had started to giggle and, finally, they'd laughed so hard that Rafe and Nick had asked them to be let in on the joke, which had only made them laugh harder.

Later, Sam saw the four of them with their heads together, deep in a low-pitched conversation that stopped abruptly when they spotted her. Her brothers-in-law—Twelves, the both of them—had colored and said hello, wasn't it a beautiful day, and Sam had known, *known*, that they were all part of the Get Samantha Married conspiracy.

The proof, if she'd needed any, had come a couple of hours later.

"You've been to Greece, haven't you, Sam?" Nick had said casually over lunch.

"Uh-huh." Sam had speared a grape tomato with her fork. "Beautiful place."

Everyone had stilled. "It is," Nick had said to the rest of the table. "A beautiful place." And they all nodded before conversation resumed.

A little while later Rafe had strolled by while she was stretched on a chaise longue, pretending to read but really napping under the hot kiss of the sun.

"So," he'd said brightly, "do you speak Greek?"

"Tourist Greek, I guess. You know, 'Where is the toilet? How much does that cost?' That kind of stuff." Sam had pushed her sunglasses down her nose and looked at him over the rims. "Why? Is there a reason I should?"

"No, no," he'd replied quickly. Too quickly. That was why warning bells rang in her head when first Carin and then Amanda just happened to stop by her room as she dressed for the party and agreed, with studied nonchalance, that it was truly a pity she didn't speak Greek because one of the guests, an old friend of Rafe's and Nick's, was from Greece.

"Well, of course, I've never met Mr. Karas but I should think he'd have appreciated it if someone spoke his language," Carin had murmured, studying her carefully manicured nails.

"Interesting," Sam had said politely. "That the gentleman should be a friend of Rafe's and Nick's and speak only Greek. I'd have thought English was sort of the *lingua franca* that the three of them would have in common."

Her sisters had tripped over their own words, hastily explaining that Demetrios Karas spoke English, of course.

"Ah," Sam had replied, as if she hadn't already figured out their plan, "is that his name? Demetrios Karas?"

Yes. It was. And he was a Shipping Magnate—Sam could almost hear the capitalization—and even though she didn't speak Greek, it would be kind of her—

"And such a help to Rafe and me," Carin had added, with a bright smile.

"—kind of you, Sam, if you'd try and make Mr. Karas feel comfortable by spending a little time with him tonight."

Sam sighed and folded her hands around her half-empty glass.

What she was going to do was make *herself* comfortable by going to her room. Tomorrow, she'd tell her sisters she'd waited as long as she could but the estimable Mr. Karas had not arrived by the time exhaustion overcame her. That much was certainly true. She had yet to spot any short, overweight, overaged Eminently Suitable shipping magnates, and she didn't want to. The probability was that she was too tired to be polite to Demetrios Karas if and when he swooped down on her.

Though, if she were in the mood, she could probably dredge up a smile for the hunk who'd wandered in a little while ago.

She wasn't. She really was tired and besides, her determined family would be watching and who knew what they'd do if they saw her flirting with a dark, dangerous, sexy stud? Still, it didn't hurt to see what he was up to... There he was, surrounded this time by a little covey of females. Two blondes, a brunette and one whose hair was highlighted so many shades that she looked like a used paintbrush. All of them were gazing up at the man as if they wanted to eat him, whole.

What a fine idea, Sam thought dreamily.

Whoops! Oh, yes. She was tired, for sure. She liked men and she liked sex, but she wasn't given to daydreaming about...

Uh-oh. Carin had just rushed into the living room. She

gave a gave a squeal of delight and launched herself at Mr. Twelve...who looked over Carin's dark head, straight at Samantha.

Sam's pulse sky-rocketed. His eyes were, indeed, the hot blue of a summer sky on the Côte d'Azur. They swept her from head to foot, then climbed again until they met hers and locked. Carin leaned back in his arms, said something. He laughed, turned his attention to her...and it was all over.

Sam let out her breath. All over? It had never been. He couldn't see her, not on the dark terrace.

She swung away, moved further into the darkness. Tired, she thought with a tiny shudder, that was what it was. Her hand trembled as she lifted her glass and brought it to her lips. It was ridiculous to feel so shaky. A good thing she was alone out here. It was a magnificent night, fragrant with flowers that bloomed in the pots set on the flagstone floor and lit by a full moon that rode high over the Brazilian prairie. Too hot, she'd heard one woman say of the weather, but to Sam it felt just right.

"Hello."

Her heart kicked against her ribs. She spun around...but it wasn't him. And it couldn't be the Greek. This was a tall, pleasant-looking guy with sandy hair. Very civilized. Civilized? What an odd distinction to attach to a person she didn't even know. Everybody here was civilized, the women in their elegant gowns, the men in their tuxes. How much more civilized could you get? Still, there was something— well, something less than civilized about the man she'd been watching, a hint of raw, even primitive power...

Sam blinked and put out her hand. "Hi. I'm Samantha Brewster."

"Nice to meet you."

"Nice to meet you, too, unless... I'm sure it's not, but just reassure me. Your name isn't Demetrios, is it?"

He laughed. "No way! I'm Jack Adams. I went to school with Nick al Rashid. And you're his sister-in-law, Samantha."

How many Eminently Suitables were wandering around tonight, Sam thought grimly, clutching her name in their reliable, stultifying hands?

"Ah," she said politely, "then you must know his wife. My sister."

Jack did. He and Sam talked about Philadelphia, where he lived, and New York, where she lived. They talked about Indonesia, where she'd just been, and New Jersey, where he'd just been. Then Jack fell silent, cleared his throat and said it would be nice to get together sometime, maybe when he was in Manhattan on business.

"I'd love to," Sam said, "but I'm hardly ever home. I do a lot of traveling."

Jack's smile turned cool. "Yeah," he said, "so I've heard." He excused himself, went inside and melted into the crowd.

Sam took a sip of her *caparhinia.*

Well, hell. She hadn't wanted to be impolite and she'd ended up being unkind, instead. She hadn't meant to be; she'd just pulled out the first excuse that came to mind but now that she thought about it, telling someone not to call you because you did a lot of traveling ranked right up there with "Sorry, but I can't see you tonight. I have to wash my hair."

It wasn't her fault. Not really. She was just wary, that was all. It was her sisters' fault. The two of them needed to start minding their own business instead of hers.

She probably shouldn't have flown down to Rio de Ouro for this party, not after three months translating Italian into English and English into Italian as the language liaison for ethnologists from Rome and San Francisco, but she hadn't wanted to miss Carin's and Rafe's fifth anniversary or her niece's fifth birthday. The two events were only separated by a few days, a fact that neither her sister nor brother-in-law ever denied, and who could blame them, when they were so obviously still crazy in love? If only Carin wasn't convinced love was the universal panacea.

"I met Rafe at a party just like this one," she'd chirped this morning.

"So did I," Amanda had chirped back. "Met Nick at a party, I mean."

Sam gave a sigh and peered into the living room again. Carin was nowhere in sight. She could chance a quick exit... But the man was still there. He was talking with someone whose name she couldn't remember. The Twelve smiled. So did the other man. They shook hands and the other guy wandered off...

Samantha's heart thudded.

There was no doubt about it. The stranger was looking at her. Directly at her, while a little smile curved over his mouth, and now he was coming towards the terrace, towards her, making his way through the crowded room...

"Demetrios!"

Sam's eyes widened. The booming voice belonged to her brother-in-law but the man who responded to it by stopping dead in his tracks and turning towards Rafe was no rotund, over-aged Lothario.

It was Mr. Twelve.

She watched, openmouthed, as he and her brother-in-law clasped hands, then laughed and threw their arms around each other in a bear hug.

"When did you get here, Demetrios?"

Demetrios. Demetrios Karas. Sam could hardly get her mind around the reality. This gorgeous creature was the man her sisters wanted her to meet? Not a toad that marriage would turn into a prince? This tall, handsome, dangerously sexy-looking man was their idea of Mister Eminently Suitable?

Only two women floating on the euphoria of wedded bliss would come up with such a plan. Demetrios Karas was no more marriage material than she was. What was that old saying? It took one to know one. Well, she knew. The man was a confirmed bachelor, a state of mind Sam understood, completely.

She stepped quickly back into the darkness and bit her lip to keep from bursting into laughter. Here she'd been skulking around because she didn't want to be shoved into the arms of someone like the professor or the rancher, men who'd expect her to cook a hot meal at the end of a long, dull day of knitting or crocheting or whatever it was the wives of men like that did and all the time her sisters' quarry had been the best-looking male on three continents.

Make that four continents.

Marriage must have turned her sisters's brains to mush.

Surely, they knew this man was not marriage material. He would cherish his freedom just as much as she cherished hers. Actually, she wouldn't even date someone like this. Oh, he might be fun for an evening but that would about do it. The smile. The swagger. He'd be self-centered, hot-tempered...and Greek. Really Greek, as in old-world, I-am-male, you-are-female, macho.

Sam rolled her eyes.

Just wait until she got hold of Carin and Amanda in the morning. Her brothers-in-law, too. And her mother, who'd done more than her fair share of trying to find her The Right Man. Get out of my life, she'd tell the bunch of them. No more matchmaking. No more setting me up. No more—

"Samantha."

Rafe purred her name in that wonderful Brazilian accent of his. Sam took a deep breath and turned towards him.

"Rafe," she said calmly. She smiled, rose on her toes and kissed his cheek. "What a lovely party."

"Carin arranged it all," he said proudly.

"Well, she did a wonderful job."

Rafe nodded. Then he tucked his hands in his trouser pockets and cleared his throat. "So. Have you met every-one?"

Here we go, she thought. "How could I?" she said, with wide-eyed innocence. "You have a zillion guests. I couldn't possibly meet everyone."

"Ah. No, of course not. But you should come inside, Sam, so you can—so you can meet some of them."

She stared at her usually unflappable brother-in-law. A flush spread across his tanned cheeks and she sighed.

"Rafe," she said gently, "I do not wish to meet Demetrios Karas."

"Carin thinks…"

"Carin should stop thinking. About me, anyway." Sam softened her words with a smile. "I'm happy as I am. Honestly."

Her brother-in-law looked relieved. "I know it. I tried telling that to her, but…"

"You didn't say anything to him, did you? To Karas?"

"Certainly not," Rafe said briskly.

"Well, that's good." Sam fluttered her lashes. "Because I'd hate to have him think of me as goods in the marketplace, if I should decide to go over and introduce myself."

"But you just said—"

"I said I didn't want to meet him. I meant as a marriage prospect." She dropped her voice to a theatrical whisper. "Actually, he wouldn't be a very good one."

"He would agree with you, I am certain," Rafe said, and smiled.

"But he'd make a great evening's entertainment."

"Samantha!"

Sam laughed. "I'm joking."

Of course she was. It was all a joke. The matchmaking. The handsome stranger with the groupies hanging all over him. The attraction she'd imagined she felt to him and the idea that he'd been looking at her. Even if he had noticed her, even if he were her type, what did it matter? She wasn't in the mood to get involved with anybody, not for an evening, not for a week, not for a long time. She wanted some peace and quiet while she came down after the months in Indonesia. Some simple translating arrangement that would keep her in New York for a bit. Then, perhaps, she'd be in the mood to meet someone and enjoy him until the next job took her someplace else.

"...if you'll forgive me."

Sam focused her eyes on Rafe. "I'm sorry. I didn't get that."

"I said I was going to find my wife and see if I can steal her for myself for a little while. That is, if you'll excuse me...?"

She smiled. "Of course. Actually, when you do find Carin, would you give her a message? Would you tell her the party's marvelous but I'm completely wiped out, and I'm going to call it a night?"

"Of course." Rafe kissed her temple. "*Boa noite,* Sam."

"Good night, Rafe."

That was precisely what she was going to do. No slinking around on the dark terrace, either. She'd go straight through the house. She'd been behaving like a schoolgirl, trying to avoid Demetrios Karas. And so much for imagining he'd been watching her, coming to claim her...

To claim her?

Sam rolled her eyes. Enough was enough. She needed a good night's sleep and she was going to get one. She smoothed back her hair, lifted her chin, put a polite smile on her face, walked briskly into the crowded living room...

And went in search of Demetrios Karas.

CHAPTER TWO

SHE was beautiful, this woman with hair the color of autumn
and eyes the deep green of the open sea.

Demetrios had noticed her as soon as he entered the room.

She was a vision of femininity in silk a shade just paler
than her eyes. A short top—cropped, his last mistress had
called the style—skimmed her breasts. Her trousers matched
the pale green top. Ordinarily, he didn't care for women in
trousers, but these...

Idly, his eyes traveled the length of her body.

These were different. They began just below her navel,
clung to her hips and thighs before falling to her ankles.
Her shoes were the same pale green and seemed to be made
of nothing but straps and slender, delicately spiked heels.

Only a saint would not have imagined her wearing just
the heels and, perhaps, a scrap or two of tantalizingly placed
lace, and no one would ever propose him for canonization.

That he should instantly envision her that way had not
surprised him. What did was the swift reaction of his body.
It was so sophomoric, so unexpected, that he'd turned away
from her, half in amusement, half in annoyance, concentrated on envisioning barren stretches of ice-choked tundra,
and plunged into conversation with a woman who'd just
called his name.

It didn't help. He said yes, no, and maybe; smiled when
it seemed a smile was appropriate, but his mind was on the
auburn-haired woman. Why was she so removed? Music
was playing, people were talking and laughing. Rafe's party
was a roaring success and yet she kept herself separate. She
stood on the threshold of the terrace, as if she couldn't decide whether she wanted to stay or leave, with a glass in

17

her hand and an indefinable look on her face. Was it boredom? Polite indifference? Whatever it was, she would have drawn every man in the room except for the way she held herself.

Keep away, her posture said, *I'm not interested.*

Still, Demetrios couldn't imagine she had come alone. Wasn't there a man with her? Each time he looked at the terrace, he saw her still standing there, alone.

The only way to get answers to his questions was to go to her and ask them. That look of world-weariness didn't put him off. On the contrary, it piqued his interest.

He waited for a lull in conversation, made an excuse and started towards her, but he didn't get very far. He knew a number of people at this party. Voices called out to him. Hands—especially female hands—reached for his arm. There was no way to avoid saying hello and yes, he was fine and no, he would not be going to Gstaad or the Canaries...or, he'd almost said to the last woman who'd batted her lashes at him, or to anyplace he was likely to run into her.

They had enjoyed each other in the past, but the affair had been over for a long time.

The redhead on the terrace didn't look like she'd cling to a man once the flame between them had died...but that was probably just wishful thinking. Experience had taught him that women were incapable of enjoying something for the moment without trying to build a life around it.

Still, it was pleasant to imagine such a possibility, the perfect woman, one who'd be as beautiful as a rare orchid and as self-sufficient as a desert cactus.

Unfortunately, such a creature had yet to be conceived. Women were either beautiful or sturdy. There was no way to blend the qualities and since he was most definitely a man who preferred beauty to durability, he'd suffered through his fair share of relationships that ended badly. More than his fair share, some might say.

Just once, Demetrios thought as the woman clinging to

his arm chattered on, just once he'd like to meet a woman who knew her own mind, who would admit to desire with honesty and forsake the need for games… And then he felt a sudden tingling. He looked up, just quickly enough to see the redhead watching him with an intensity that made him want to push past the idiotic female babbling at him, shoulder through the crowd, take the redhead in his arms and carry her off.

Of course, he hadn't done it. Civilized men didn't do such things.

So he waited, ended the conversation and started towards her again, but the fates were against him. When Rafe called his name, what else could he do but respond? They'd been friends for years. Still, once they'd gone through the hellos and how have you beens, Demetrios decided to be blunt. You could do that, with a man.

"Rafe," he said, with a little smile, "let's catch up on old times later. Tomorrow, perhaps. How does that sound?"

Rafe grinned and clapped him on the back. "It sounds as if you have your eye on someone. Who is she?"

Demetrios grinned, too. "I don't know her name yet. I've only seen her."

"Well, point her out. What sort of friend would I be if I couldn't help?"

"She's right…" There, he started to say, but she wasn't. He glimpsed a flash of green silk, nothing more. The mystery woman had faded into the darkness of the terrace. "She *was* right there. Never mind." He smiled. "There are some things a man should do for himself."

"And I'm sure you'll succeed," Rafe said, smiling back. "Nick says you used to put him to shame, in the old days."

"I'm glad he admits it, but then, he's an old married man now."

"Happily married," Rafe said, and cleared his throat. "As I am. And I'm sure you will be, too, when you find the right woman."

Demetrios could almost hear his mental alarm start ringing. The expression on Rafe's face had become serious. No, he thought, no. Surely a friend would not try to…

"So," Rafe said, far too briskly, "have you met all my wife's family?"

"Marriage has dulled your brain." Demetrios grinned. "I've done business with Jonas, remember? At Espada, where I met his wife and sons. And, of course, I know Nick's Amanda, and your beautiful Carin."

"Then, uh, then the only one of the Barons you haven't met is Sam."

"Sam?" Demetrios frowned. "I don't recall Jonas having a son named Sam."

"No, no. Sam is short for Samantha."

"Ah," Demetrios said, as if he understood when, in fact, he hadn't the slightest idea what his friend was talking about. "I knew the old man had a stepdaughter, but—"

"Sam isn't Jonas's daughter." Rafe cleared his throat again. "Samantha isn't actually a Baron. She is a Brewster. My wife's youngest sister."

"Ah," Demetrios said again, and glanced towards the terrace. Was she still out there? She had to be. He had to meet her. In a room filled with beauty, hers had shone as brightly as the beacon that marked the anchorage of his private island in the Aegean. "Rafe, my friend—"

"Sam is here, somewhere. Why don't you let me find her and introduce you?"

Hell. That was what this was all about. Rafael Alvares, who bred world-class horses and captained a Brazilian financial empire, had been given the role of matchmaker. It was pathetic, what happened to a man, once a woman put a ring through his nose.

"That sounds, uh, it sounds wonderful," Demetrios said heartily. "But, ah, but I have to step out for a moment." He patted the pocket where he kept his cell phone. "I have to, uh, to make a call to New York. And it's so noisy in here…"

"You'll like her. I know you will."

"Yes. Well, I'm sure I would, but—"

"She's your type of woman."

"Really." Demetrios raised an eyebrow.

"Absolutely. You might not think so, at first. Sam is a challenge."

Meaning, she was bad-tempered.

"She's hot-tempered, with a mind of her own."

Meaning, no man had yet been found who could tolerate her. Demetrios had come to understand the language of those who wanted to end his happy bachelorhood. That the words should spew from the mouth of a friend didn't make them any less deadly.

"She sounds…fascinating," he said politely. "And I'm certain she is as beautiful as your wife."

Rafe seemed to think about it. "No," he said, after a minute, "I must admit, Sam doesn't look anything like Carin. She doesn't look like Amanda, either."

Worse and worse. His old friend was trying to fix him up with an over-the-hill grouch who bore a man's name and had none of the beauty of her sisters.

"Well," Demetrios said, lying through his teeth, "she sounds delightful—but I have to make that call. And I see some people I know. Let me make the call, say hello, and then I'll certainly get back to you so you can introduce me to your sister-in-law."

Rafe sighed. "No, you won't."

"Don't give me that look. I'm not trying to, ah, to avoid meeting this—this paragon. I simply—"

"You're simply not ready to lose your beloved freedom." Rafe's sigh became a smile. "It's all right, Demetrios. I said as much to Carin, but she insisted you and Sam would be a perfect match. What can I tell you, my friend? You know how women are."

"All too well," Demetrios said, sighing with relief. "That's why I'm happy to remain single."

Rafe walked away. He started towards the terrace only to

be waylaid yet again, this time by a blonde with whom he'd had a long-forgotten liaison.

"Darling," she squealed, and he kissed her cheek when she tilted her face to his, but there was a limit to his patience.

"Forgive me," he said, with a show of teeth he hoped would appear to be a smile, "but I really must—"

And then a hint of fragrance drifted towards him. Jasmine? Lilac?

"Hello."

The voice was soft, husky, and touched with amusement. Demetrios felt all his senses go on alert. Only one woman at this party had the power to turn him on with a simple word; he knew, instantly, it was she. He turned slowly, wondering if the reality of her would match his fantasies...

Yes. God, yes. She was more than beautiful. She was magnificent. Eyes a man could get lost in. A mouth that begged to be kissed. Hair that glinted with the fire of the sun.

"How lovely you are," he said softly.

She laughed. "How direct *you* are."

"I've been watching you. And you've been watching me. Why should either of us pretend?" He moved a step closer. "I've spent the entire evening trying to get to your side."

She smiled and held out a glass. Until then, he hadn't even noticed that she held one in each hand, both filled with crushed ice and pale golden liquid.

"In that case, you must be thirsty."

Demetrios smiled. "Don't tell me...*caparhinias?*"

"I thought you asked me not to tell you." Their fingers brushed as he took one of the glasses from her and a charge of electricity flashed through him. Through her, too. He saw her eyes suddenly darken and knew she must have felt the same hot surge. "Do you like what I've brought you, Mr. Karas?"

"Yes," he said in a low voice, his eyes locked on hers,

knowing she wasn't talking about the *caparhinias*. "Very much."

"Good." She smiled, lifted her drink to her lips and took a sip of the sugary rum concoction. "I thought you might."

She was a flirt. A tease. And yet, she was blunt about what she wanted. The combination was dazzling. He wanted to take her into his arms, carry her through the house, up the stairs to his bed...

"Demetrios?" a voice behind him whined.

Hell. "One moment," he said softly, and turned to the blonde. "I'm sorry," he said politely. "But I'm busy."

He was being rude. He knew it, but he didn't care. All that mattered was the woman...

She was gone. But where? The terrace. Yes. He saw a flash of green silk being swallowed up by the darkness. He put his glass on a table and shouldered his way through the crowd, ignoring everything but the woman.

There she was, hurrying down the wide steps that led to the gently sloping lawn.

"Wait!"

Her pace quickened, until she was almost running. Demetrios cursed, went after her, caught her as she reached a shadowed gazebo. He clasped her shoulders and swung her towards him. Moonlight lit her face.

"Why did you run away? Are you afraid of me?" Gently, he cupped her face in his hands, his fingers stroking the curve of her cheekbones. "There's no reason to be. I won't hurt you."

Sam stared up at him. There was no way to explain. What could she tell him? That she'd only been teasing, at first, because it was fun to know she'd been coming on to the evening's unknowing quarry? That what had started as fun had changed? That she could imagine going to bed with him, wanted to go to bed with him, but that not even she, for all her talk, fell into bed so fast? It was out of the question anyway. Her entire family had pointed her in his direction. She doubted if he'd want to hear that.

Sam moistened her lips. "I'm sorry if I misled you. But I'm—I'm tired. And—"

"And, you don't know me. That's the problem, isn't it?" His gaze fell to her lips, then rose. "You could know me," he said softly. "One kiss. That is all it would take, and then we would both know all we need to know."

"I don't think—"

"Don't think. Not tonight."

Slowly, he lowered his head to hers. Despite his words, she knew he was giving her time to end the game before it was too late.

His eyes were pools of indigo, half shielded by thick, black lashes.

I could drown in his eyes, she thought, and then his mouth brushed hers like a whisper of moonlight, brushed it again and again, and with a little sigh, Sam gave up thinking, closed her eyes, parted her lips and welcomed his kiss.

He tasted of wine and of moonlight, of a thousand forgotten dreams and of a quest that had never quite been fulfilled. And despite everything, she knew, as he kissed her, that she wanted more.

Unbidden, the word whispered from her lips. "More."

Demetrios groaned. More. Yes. He would give her more. He would give her everything, take everything. He brought her closer, slipped his hands up her throat, felt the urgent pulsing of her blood, cupped her face and lifted it to his.

Samantha leaned into him, wanting the feel of him against her breasts, her belly, her thighs. He slid his hands down her shoulders and she trembled at the rough brush of his fingers against her bare skin, moaned when he gathered her tightly in his arms.

Her hands lifted, wrapped around his neck, and he knew she was surrendering herself to him, to the night, to passion. He bit lightly at her bottom lip, then soothed the tiny hurt with his tongue. She tasted of rum and sugar, of heat and desire, and he groaned again and fell back against the wall, taking her with him, sweeping his hand possessively down her body. He cupped her breast, swallowed her cry as the silk-covered nipple rose against his palm, curved his hand around her hip.

"Matya mou," he said thickly, turning so that their positions were reversed and it was she who leaned against the gazebo. He moved into the vee of her legs and she arched against him, moved against him, and he knew he was as close to losing himself as he had ever been in all the years since he'd left boyhood behind.

"Wait," he whispered, but she was touching him, sliding her hands under his jacket, tearing at his shirt so that the studs popped free and fell to the ground. He caught his breath at the feel of her cool fingers against his skin, and he clasped her wrists in one hand while he stepped back and tried to regain his sanity, but she gave a little whimper of distress that fueled his hunger. He understood her need. It was the same for him, the urgency to touch and taste that was almost pain, but he would not permit himself such a total loss of control. He could wait. He would take her where there was privacy, where there was a bed, a place to be alone.

He brushed a light kiss on her swollen mouth and wound his fingers through hers.

"My room," he said, but she shook her head wildly.

"No. Not in the house. I can't—I don't—"

She didn't want to run the risk of seeing people. God knew, neither did he. "The stables," he said, and before she could reply, he led her from the gazebo towards the outbuildings.

"Wait," she said, just as he had moments before, and he thought she had changed her mind, thought what he would do if she had, but she stopped only long enough to kick off her shoes. He scooped them up and they ran through the damp grass side by side. She was laughing softly, and he stopped, swung her into his arms and kissed her.

A cloud hid the moon, leaving the sky touched only with the fire of the stars, but Demetrios knew his way. There was a small office just off the stables. He and Rafe had sealed a deal in it. It was not elaborate. A desk. A chair. A couch. An old leather couch. Not big, but big enough for a man and a woman to make love.

He would take her there, undress her, sink into the lushness of her mouth, into the heat of her body. With the first frantic hunger eased, he would hold her in his arms, caress her. The crowd would thin, the party would end, and they would go to the house then, to his room, lose themselves in each other through the long, hot Brazilian night.

The stable was dark and pleasantly scented with horse and leather. An animal snorted as the door swung shut behind them.

Demetrios drew Samantha towards the office at the rear of the building.

"Demetrios?" she whispered.

"Yes," he said thickly. She knew his name? He didn't know hers. He thought of asking, but what did it matter at this moment? Instead, he took her hand, brought it to his erection. "Feel what you do to me, *o kalóz mou.*" He heard her breath catch as her fingers curled over his hardness.

"Feel what you do to *me,*" she said, and she lifted his hand to her breast.

Her silk-covered nipple, hard as a pearl, pressed against his palm. He groaned, kissed her deeply, savoring the sweetness of her mouth while he drew her down onto the couch and gathered her into his arms. She moaned, pressed fevered kisses to his jaw, wound her arms around his neck and, for a heartbeat, the frenzy within him eased. He felt a sudden need to hold her, just hold her, to learn the sweet secrets of her body before slaking his desire.

"Tell me your name," he said softly. "I want to know—"

Impatiently, she moved against him, moved again, and he was lost. He slid his hand along the warm, exposed flesh between her breasts and her navel, eased his hand under the waistband of her trousers, down and down, groaning at the first brush of silken curls, capturing her mouth with his when she cried out…

Lights blazed on in the stable. The woman in his arms froze. "Oh, God," she said in a frantic whisper, and her sinuous movements turned to frenzied attempts to push him away. "Get off me! Don't you see the lights? Someone is—"

"Shh." He put his lips to her ear. "Don't talk. Whoever it is will leave."

Leave? Sam squeezed her eyes shut. Please, yes. They had to leave…

"…delighted you are prepared to make up your mind about the colt, Nick," Rafe Alvares said, and chuckled. "I have had an offer. An excellent one, and I'm tempted to accept it."

"The hell you will," Nicholas al Rashid replied, with lazy humor. "Doesn't being your brother-in-law count for anything?"

Both men laughed. Their footsteps sounded on the planked floor. Sam buried her face in Demetrios's throat.

"There he is. A fine animal. As handsome as ever."

Nick sighed. "More handsome than ever. All right. It's a deal. Ship him to my farm in Greenwich."

"As soon as I can make the arrangements."

"They'll go now," Demetrios whispered—and followed it with an oath. He was wrong. The men weren't leaving. The footsteps were drawing closer. Closer…

He sat up quickly, whipped off his jacket and draped it around Sam's shoulders. Then he shot to his feet and stood in front of her, blocking her from view.

The light in the little office came on. "Let's celebrate," Rafe said, "with a brandy. Or would you prefer… Demetrios?"

"Demetrios?" Nick said, his voice a puzzled echo of Rafe's. There was a moment's silence, and then he cleared his throat. "Oh."

Oh, indeed, Sam thought, and wished, with all her heart, that she were dead.

"Have we, uh, have we interrupted something?"

She squeezed her eyes shut in an old parody of the children's game. If she couldn't see them, they couldn't see her. They really couldn't, she told herself frantically. Demetrios hadn't moved. He was a protective wall, and she was huddled deep in his jacket with her knees drawn up, her face buried against them, but she had never felt more exposed in her life.

"Let's step outside," he said. There was a shuffle of feet, the creak of the door half closing, then the sound of Demetrios's voice saying calmly, almost lazily, "Actually, you have interrupted something," as if were all some sort of joke.

Sam curled her hands into fists.

"Damn," Nick murmured. "Sorry, Karas."

Sam's heart pounded like a drum. *Go away. Go away. Go away!*

Rafe cleared his throat. "I had no idea that you—that you were…" He cleared his throat again. "Well. I can see why you didn't want to meet my wife's sis… Damn! Never mind."

"Right," Nick said quickly, "never mind. We'll see you later, Demetrios. Rafe? Let's go."

Sam held her breath until she heard the footsteps recede. The lights went off, the door banged shut and she scrambled to her feet just as Demetrios hurried towards her.

"Kalóz mou," he said, reaching for her…

She slammed a fist against his chest. "Don't—don't *'kalóz mou'* me! And don't touch me, either!"

"Sweetheart. I am sorry. I regret that we were interrupted, but—"

"Yes. I'll just bet you do."

She glared at him, her blood hot with rage. He was talking in a soft, soothing voice, trying to talk her back onto that couch, but that wasn't going to happen. How could she have done this? She'd almost slept with a stranger—a stranger who hadn't wanted to meet her. Wasn't that what Rafe had just said? That Demetrios hadn't wanted to meet his wife's sister?

The man who'd almost bedded her hadn't wanted to meet her. Okay, he didn't know she was the woman he hadn't wanted to meet. Maybe that made a difference. Maybe her logic was flawed but dammit, who cared about logic? She'd been humiliated, embarrassed...and the man who was arrogance and self-conceit personified was still talking.

"Oh, shut up," Sam said, and brushed past him. She tried to, anyway, but he put out his arm and stopped her.

"Have you heard a thing I said?"

His faint accent, so softly sexy a little while ago, had thickened. Sam blew her hair back from her forehead.

"This is all your fault. If you were any kind of gentleman—"

"Ah. I see. You wish to pretend you had no part in this."

"I'm not the one who dragged me into this—this barn."

"One," he said coldly, "it is a stable. Two, if I were not a gentleman, there might be some debate as to who dragged who."

"Whom," Sam snapped.

"Three," Demetrios said, his voice cutting across hers, "we are only here because you refused to go into the house."

"Yes. Yes, I did. I, at least, have some sense of propriety."

"That is surely the reason you climbed all over me at the gazebo."

He wasn't just arrogant, he was insufferable. Sam thought about slapping him but really, he wasn't worth the effort. Exhaustion, she thought furiously, as she pushed past him and headed for the stable door. It was all a case of exhaustion.

"You have my jacket," he said sharply. "Or are you in the habit of taking souvenirs?"

She swung towards him and flung a string of curses she'd just learned in Egypt in his face. Demetrios glowered; a horse in a nearby stall gave a soft whinny and looked on with interest.

"What did you say?"

"I said," Sam replied, smiling brightly, "that I hoped your descendents would all be carrion-eating jackals, and that you'd lose all your teeth and go bald by the time you're thirty-five. Good night. I'd say it's been a pleasure, but it hasn't."

"You're right. It hasn't."

"As for your precious jacket…" She shrugged the item in question from her shoulders and held it out in a two-fingered grasp. Demetrios looked from her face to the jacket to the horse in its stall…

"No," he said, but it was too late. The jacket dropped. The horse snorted. And the woman he'd been fool enough to have thought he wanted strode towards the door.

"Good night," Sam said pleasantly, and batted the door open with her hand.

A single, harsh word floated out into the night. It was Greek, but she didn't have to be a genius to figure out what it meant. Sam dusted her hands off as she strode towards the house. The jacket had, undoubtedly, found its hoped-for target, something that was the inevitable product of horses and stables.

There was justice in this world after all.

Demetrios glared at the closed door. Then, teeth clenched, he leaned into the stall and carefully retrieved his jacket. He carried it as the woman had, by two fingers, until he reached the door where he dropped it into a trash container.

He had never learned her name, but it wasn't necessary. As far as he was concerned, it might as well be Circe. She was a sorceress. A tease. Hell, she was a bitch… And yet, as he stepped out into the warm night and thought of the curses she'd uttered, his lips began to twitch.

Descendents that were jackals were bad enough, but that

he should be toothless and bald in another two years? He began to chuckle, and then to laugh out loud. She was not the first woman to have cursed him, though it had always been because he was the one heading for the door. Certainly, none had ever done it so creatively.

As for Nick and Rafe... Demetrios sighed. He was going to have to come up with some kind of explanation. He was sure they'd be waiting for him. They'd want details, the name of the woman, why he'd taken her to the stables instead of to his bedroom...

Why he'd had to dump his jacket in the trash.

Well, they were in for a disappointment. He wasn't going to tell them much of anything. The assignation—the *almost* assignation—had begun as passion and ended as farce, but he had no wish to share it, not even for the good-natured laughter it would surely bring. It had been far too private.

As for Circe...whoever she was, she was quite a woman.

Whistling softly, even smiling—which, he had to admit, was an odd thing to do, considering the less than satisfactory end to what had begun as a fascinating evening—Demetrios tucked his hands into his pockets and strolled towards the house.

CHAPTER THREE

ALMOST four weeks later, the phone in Sam's apartment rang just as she was pouring her first cup of morning coffee.

She put down the pot, glanced at the clock and picked up the receiver. "Good morning, Amanda," she said sweetly.

Her sister gave a dramatic groan. "Please don't tell me they've perfected video calling. Not at this hour of the morning."

Sam laughed. "This hour of the morning is how I knew it was you. Nobody else would call me at five after seven."

"Anybody with a four-year-old would. Besides, I wanted to be sure and get you before you left for the day. Didn't you say you had a job interview on tap?"

"Two of them," Sam said, tucking the phone against her shoulder so she could open the fridge and get out the cream. "The first one's in just a couple of hours, so—"

"So, you can't talk long. Yes, I know. That's been your excuse ever since we got back from Brazil."

"It isn't an excuse," Sam said quickly. Too quickly, she thought, and told herself to slow down. "I've been busy, that's all."

"Uh-huh. Well, what's on that frantic schedule of yours today?"

"A couple of meetings this morning. Which means—"

"Which means," Amanda said pleasantly, "you and I can get together for lunch. Remember that little place off Madison?"

"Where walking through the door and inhaling puts a thousand calories on your hips?"

"Haven't you heard the latest scientific facts, sister mine?

32

A blast of sunshine reduces the calorie count. And, in case you haven't noticed, spring has finally sprung. Take a peep out your window. That big yellow ball hanging over the East River is sun.''

"It's pollution. And honestly, Mandy, I don't see how I can make it. I'm seeing somebody at the UN at nine—''

"You're going to work at the United Nations? I thought you hated being bottled up indoors.''

"It's a private job. Some letters that need translating. And then, at eleven, there's a professor at Hunter who stumbled across some poems by a nineteenth century—''

"Fascinating,'' Amanda said politely. "But I thought you didn't do that. Translate poetry and letters, I mean. I thought you preferred on-the-spot things. You know, Mr. Pavarotti, meet Mr. Jagger. That kind of stuff.''

Sam laughed as she stirred a dollop of cream into her coffee. "Well, that's what I prefer, but my bank account isn't as finicky as my brain—especially when I haven't picked up a decent job since—since I got back from that weekend at Carin's.''

What an idiot! Surely, after all this time, she could trust herself to say "Brazil'' without dredging up memories of that humiliating episode with Demetrios Karas.

"Really?''

"Really. Nobody seems to need translations in French or German or Italian or Spanish or—''

"Borneoese?''

Sam laughed again. "You just invented a language. Anyway, what I did in Borneo was translate from Italian to English and from English to Italian. There was this pair of ethnologists, see, and one spoke...'' She sighed. "Trust me. I don't do what you just dubbed Borneoese.''

"Or Greek,'' Amanda said pleasantly.

Every nerve cell in Sam's body went on alert. "Why would I need to speak Greek?''

"You wouldn't. I just mentioned it. I mean, you said—"

"I know what *I* said. And what *you* said. And you said, Greek."

"Samantha, honestly, stop being so defensive. Have you had your morning coffee?"

Sam stared down into her rapidly cooling cup. "No."

"Well, you see? That's what you get for trying to talk to me before you get your caffeine levels where they should be."

"Amanda. *You* are the one who called me."

"So I did, although I don't know why you should be such a grump, considering that I'm inviting you to a sinfully scrumptious lunch where I'm going to tell you about your next job."

Sam stood up straight. "Translating?"

"Of course. What other kind of job would Nick offer you?"

"Your husband needs a translator?"

"A business acquaintance of his needs one. Well, actually, a friend. And it's your kind of thing, Sam, nothing to do with dusty old letters or poetry."

"Well, that's great!" Sam lifted her cup and drank some coffee. "Who'll I be working with? Where? In what languages?"

"I don't really know the details. You can get all that from Nick. He said he'd meet us at The Lazy Daisy and fill you in."

"Okay. Fine." Sam cleared her throat. "Uh, so, speaking of Nick... Did he, um, did he enjoy the weekend at Rio de Ouro?"

"Doesn't he always? You know what good friends he and Rafe are."

"Oh, sure." Sam ran the tip of her tongue over her lips. "And—and I'm sure he saw other friends that weekend, too.

I mean, they all know each other, don't they? Nick. Rafe. And—and other people.''

"All of a sudden, I have the feeling I'm the one in need of a translator. What are you talking about?''

What, indeed? Sam shut her eyes and rubbed a finger across the bridge of her nose. If Demetrios Karas had figured out who she was, if he'd told either of her brothers-in-law about his—his encounter with her, she'd have known it. Rafe and Nick would have confronted her like the protective big brothers they'd become.

By now, her sisters and their husbands would have been all over her.

No, her family was clueless and they were going to stay that way. What had happened was history, and so was Demetrios Karas. Just thinking it made the day improve.

"Sam?''

"You don't need a translator,'' Sam said briskly. "It's me. I need that caffeine you mentioned before I can carry on even a halfway intelligent conversation. I'll see you at The Lazy Daisy.''

"Wonderful. I'll reserve a table in the solarium so we can enjoy this gorgeous sunshine.''

But by late morning, the sun had gone into hiding.

The sky was a leaden gray when Sam hurried towards Hunter College for her appointment; by the time she left the college, it was raining. Fat drops pattered against the pavement as thunder rolled across the city. Sam eyed the traffic, but she knew better than to stand around and get wet in the futile hope of snagging a taxi. Someday, somebody would solve the mystery and figure out where cabs hid when the weather turned soggy. In the meantime, there was no choice but to make a run for the restaurant.

She was thoroughly drenched when she finally ducked under The Lazy Daisy's royal-blue canopy. The captain hurried towards her as she stepped through the smoked-glass doors.

"I'm meeting someone," Sam said, out of breath from the mad sprint.

"Certainly, Miss Brewster."

She caught a glimpse of herself in the mirrored walls as he helped her out of her coat. What a mess! She had a faint resemblance to something left too long in the wet, but it didn't matter. She'd already finished her business appointments. Neither Amanda nor Nick would care if she looked like something the cat had dragged in.

"This way, please, Miss Brewster. Her Highness is waiting for you."

Sam fell in behind the captain and tried not to grin. She had no illusions about him remembering her from a visit nearly six months earlier. It was Amanda's presence that had done it. Her sister didn't actually have a title, not since Nick had renounced the throne of his homeland, but you couldn't tell that to some of the world-class snobs who became New York head waiters.

Despite the rain, Amanda had taken a table in the solarium as she'd promised. The rest of the area was deserted. Evidently, nobody else wanted to sit inside a glass room while rain poured from the skies but the scene was cozy enough and Amanda looked warm and content as she sat in a candle-lit booth.

She waved when she saw Sam. "There you are," she said happily, rising so they could exchange hugs. They sat down, smiling at each other, talking about Amanda's children, Sam's much-loved nephew and niece, pausing only when the *sommelier* appeared with a bottle of wine.

"I ordered a syrah," Amanda said. "Is that okay with you? I figured red wine goes with cool, wet weather."

"Uh-huh." Sam smiled. "So does sitting underwater in a solarium."

"Do you mind? It's so private, and besides, there's something wonderfully decadent about... Oh, Sam. Just look at your hair!"

"Fortunately," Sam said dryly, "I don't have to. You're the one stuck with the view of me masquerading as Medusa."

"I didn't mean that, and you know it. All those curls... It's glorious! You ought to wear it this way all the time. It's so sexy."

Gravely, the *sommelier* offered Amanda the cork. She smiled and waved it away. "I trust you, George," she said. "Just pour, please. My sister and I are parched." When the glasses were filled, she leaned forward. "How'd your appointments go?"

Sam sighed, lifted her glass and took an appreciative sip. "Let's put it this way. It's a good thing Nick has a job for me."

"Nothing panned out, huh?"

"Well, the guy at the UN turned out to be the second assistant to the first assistant to...." Sam made a face. "Oh, what's the difference? The bottom line is that he's developed a thing for a secretary in the French delegation, and he thought it would be cool if I'd write maybe a dozen love letters for him."

"He wanted you to write love letters for him?" Amanda stared over the rim of her glass. "As in, you're Cyrano and he's whoever the other guy was in that old play?"

"Uh-huh. He couldn't believe it when I said thanks but no thanks, that I was a translator, not a Miss Lonely Hearts who wrote letters for the lovelorn." Sam drank some more of her wine. "So, then I went to see the guy with the poems. Only it turned out he doesn't have poems."

"No?"

"No. He has *a* poem."

"*A* poem, as in one?"

"Yup. A sonnet. Fourteen lines, written by some obscure Spanish poet in the nineteen twenties. How long would it take me to translate it? he asked. How about you ask someone in the Spanish department? I answered. Better half a minute of their time than mine."

"Do I detect a touch of bitterness?" Amanda said, arching a delicate eyebrow.

Sam dug into her purse, took out her appointment list and tore it in half. "Two meetings. An entire morning. And what do I have to show for it? *Nada. Niente. Nichts.*"

Amanda winced. "It's a good thing I'm buying lunch."

"It's even better that you have a job to offer me. Do you know any of the details? I mean, if some bozo's going to push a memo under my nose, ask me to translate it..."

"No, no. I'm sure it's more involved than that. Nick said this might take weeks, even months, something about an international conglomerate. French money, Italian money... Who knows what?" She sat back, smiling, as their waiter handed them oversize menus. "Sounds as if it's right up your alley."

"The man's a friend of Nick's?"

"Uh-huh. Mmm. What'll we have? The duck is wonderful here."

"Foreign?"

"I don't think so," Amanda said, her eyes still on the menu. "Isn't the best duck usually local? From Long Island?"

A chill tiptoed up Sam's spine. Her sister was up to something. The only question was, What? "Amanda?"

"Yes?"

"Why won't you talk about this man?"

"I told you. I don't have details. Ah. They have seared scallops. I just love—"

"You must know something. Is he an American? Or is he a foreigner?"

"Both, actually." Amanda lifted the menu higher. All Sam could see of her sister was the top of her head. "Which shall I have, the duck or the scallops? Decisions, decisions." Her tone was artificially bright. "I know," she said, folding the menu and waving for the waiter. "We'll get both, and we can share."

Sam paid no attention as her sister placed the order. Why should she suddenly think of Demetrios Karas? She'd thought of him before, far too often, but always when there was time to relish how he'd looked when she'd dropped his jacket into that stall. Why think of him now, in the midst of what was going to be a pleasant lunch?

"Well," Amanda said briskly, "that's done. Now tell me how you've been. And what you've been doing, who you've been seeing—"

"Answer the question, please. Who's the man who needs a translator?"

"I told you. A friend of—"

"Am I supposed to believe that he's nameless?"

"Sam." Amanda leaned forward. "Cross my heart and hope to die—"

"That's what you always said when we were kids and you were about to tell me a lie."

"For goodness' sake," Amanda said with indignation, "we aren't kids anymore. Besides, you made it perfectly clear that night at Carin's that the last person in the world you wanted to bother with was Demetrios Karas, so why on earth would I try and set you up with him again?"

Sam stared at her sister. "I didn't mention Demetrios Karas."

Amanda blinked. "Didn't you? I could have sworn you just said—"

"I didn't," Sam said flatly.

"Well." Amanda smiled, picked up her glass, then put it down. "Well, you said you thought I was trying to fix you up. And I guess I just thought of the last time that happened. And—''

"Actually," Sam said softly, her gaze fixed on her sister, "I didn't say that, either. I simply asked who it was that needed a translator. You were the one who started babbling about not fixing me up with the highly esteemed Mr. Karas."

"Really, Sam—''

"Really, Amanda. What's going on?''

"Nothing. For goodness' sake, here I am, trying to give you some good news—''

"What does it have to do with that man?''

"What... Ah. Here's our lunch.''

Deftly, Amanda divided the scallops and the slices of duck breast. Sam watched her through narrowed eyes.

"You know what man," she said, after a few minutes. "Demetrios Karas." Her sister's face went from pale pink to deep rose. It was not, Sam thought coldly, a good sign. "This *is* about him, isn't it?''

Amanda sighed, put down her knife and fork and touched her napkin to her lips. "Look, you're making a big deal out of nothing. Yes, okay. What happened was, Nick had dinner with Demetrios a couple of nights ago. And Demetrios said—''

"Whatever he said, it was a lie!''

"For goodness' sake. Why would Demetrios lie?''

"I didn't even tell him my name!''

"What?''

"Did he describe me to Nick? Did Nick figure out that...? Amanda. The man's a liar.''

"But why would he lie? Honestly, Samantha—''

"Oh, that's it. Take his side instead of mine.''

"Will you calm down?" Amanda looked around them, then leaned over the table. "I don't know what you're talking about.''

"I want nothing to do with Demetrios Karas! I don't like him. And I especially don't like being set up by my very own sister." Sam plunked her napkin on the table. "Enjoy your lunch. I'm out of here."

"Are you nuts?" Amanda grabbed Sam's wrist as she began to slide across the booth. "You're acting like…" She paused, cocked her head. "You don't like him? But you said you'd never met him."

"Never mind what I said. I'm telling you that I want nothing to do with—"

"Uh, am I interrupting something?"

Sam jerked her head up. Nicholas al Rashid stood beside their table, a smile on his handsome face. A tentative smile, anyway, Sam thought furiously. Maybe he wasn't as dense as his wife. Maybe he'd already figured out that she wasn't to be played with.

"Nick," Amanda said, and let out a breath. "Darling, would you please tell my sister that she's behaving like an idiot?"

"Nicholas," Sam said curtly, "whose idea was this? Amanda's? Or yours?"

Nick gave his wife a bewildered look. "What's she talking about?"

"I don't know. I started to tell her about Demetrios and she exploded."

Sam tugged her hand free, shot to her feet and glared at Nick. "Actually, I don't care whose idea it was. You can just tell Demetrios Karas that—"

"Tell him what?" a voice said, and Sam froze. There was only one man who could take a couple of simple words and make them sound as if he were murmuring them into a sated woman's ear as she lay in his arms.

Please, she thought, *oh please, let this not be happening. Let the floor open and swallow me whole…*

But it was happening. Demetrios Karas had joined Nick

beside the table. Sam held her breath. His gaze swept over her, moved past her to Amanda…and returned to fix on her face. She'd always wondered if people's jaws really dropped in astonishment. Now, looking at him, she knew that they did.

He was as stunned to see her as she was to see him.

Then—then, nobody knew what had happened. Not Nick. Not Amanda. Her knees went weak with relief, but it was short-lived. They *would* know, in a couple of minutes.

"Sam?" Nick said softly.

Her brother-in-law slid his arm around her waist. She looked up at him, heart thumping.

"You okay?" he murmured.

She nodded. "Yes. I'm fine. I just…"

Just what? She had only two choices, turn tail and run or stick out the next embarrassing moments. There was no real choice. She'd never run from anything in her life…anything but this man. All these weeks, she'd told herself she'd come to her senses that night and put a stop to what had been about to happen. Now, faced with the living, breathing reality of Demetrios Karas, she was forced to admit the truth.

Fate had permitted her to escape him that night, but it wasn't going to give her a second chance. She was going to have to deal with this and do it without flinching.

"Nick," she said, on a deep breath. "Mandy. I know you meant well, but—"

"So, Nicholas. You told me your sister-in-law was a talented linguist. You neglected to mention that she is also a beautiful woman."

Sam blinked. Demetrios had recovered his composure. The self-confident smile was back—but the glitter in his eyes was hard as ice.

"Save your breath," she said coolly. "I'm not that easy to impress."

The intake of Amanda's breath seemed to echo in the room. "Sam!" she hissed, but Demetrios laughed.

"And she is direct, too. How charming."

"This man and I already know each other," Sam said. Her chin lifted. "And he's wasting his time if he thinks he can make me think anything less of him than I already do."

"Surely," Demetrios said, his smile fading, "the lady will accept my apologies for what happened that night at Rio de Ouro."

"Rio de Ouro?" Amanda looked from Demetrios to Sam. "Do you two know each other? Sam? You never said anything. I mean, all of us wanted—we hoped—and now it turns out—it turns out—"

"Perhaps I've given the wrong impression." Demetrios's voice was smooth as silk. "We met, but only briefly. And, before we really got to know each other, I was, ah, distracted. By the time I returned, your sister was gone. Isn't that right, Samantha?"

What kind of game was he playing? "No," Sam said, glaring at him. "And it's Miss Brewster."

"Sam," Amanda said nervously, "what's the matter with you? Demetrios, really, I apologize. My sister's had a, uh, a difficult day. She went on two job interviews—"

"Amanda!"

"—two interviews, one with a guy who wanted her to write love letters for him and another with some jerk who had a poem to translate. Both job offers were so much below her capability that it's pathetic." Amanda flashed a wary look at her sister. "Isn't that right, Sam?"

"Those interviews have nothing to do with this," Sam said coldly.

"I would hope not." Demetrios's smile tilted. "It would be unfortunate if Samantha...sorry. If Miss Brewster were to let her disappointment over her morning affect her dealings with me."

Nick and Amanda looked from Demetrios to Sam. They might as well have been at a tennis match, Sam thought bitterly. And, in a way, they were right. Demetrios had just sent her a wicked backhand shot. He'd woven a story that sounded plausible, if you didn't think too much about it. She was a woman with a dented ego; he was a man who'd become inattentive. The self-deprecation was enough to make her want to be sick or to slug him, especially now that he'd added a threat so well-disguised that nobody but she would recognize it for what it was.

Still, the bottom line was that he'd chosen to keep their secret, and heaven knew that was better than blurting out the sleazy truth.

Why had he lied? She wasn't fool enough to think it had anything to do with his being a gentleman. He wasn't. He was a rogue in a custom-made suit and yes, maybe that was part of what had attracted her to him that night, but that nonsense was long past.

Wasn't it?

She shivered. Nick, who still held her in a loose embrace, gave her a quick hug. "Cold?"

"No," she said brightly, "I'm not. I'm just—I'm just—"

"She's just still hungry," Amanda said quickly. She flashed a smile around the little group. "We were about to order dessert when you guys showed up."

"I am not the least bit interested in dessert. And I don't think—"

"Don't think," Demetrios smiled lazily, just as he had that night. "Women always think too much, when it comes to things that bring pleasure." His eyes met hers. "Like dessert," he said smoothly. He moved closer, linked his hand through hers. She jerked at his touch and his fingers tightened on hers in silent warning. "Coffee and something sweet sounds like a fine idea. And then, after your sister and brother-in-law leave, we can have a second cup of coffee and discuss my need for your services.''

"I have no intention of—"

"You know," Amanda said briskly, "I really don't want any dessert. Nick? Darling? How about you?"

"Well," Nick said, looking bewildered, "actually, I thought I might even have a sand…" His voice trailed off as he met his wife's gaze. "No. No, I don't."

"In fact," Amanda said, "we have to leave. We have an appointment."

"Right," Nick stammered, "right. An appointment. How could I have forgotten?"

They were lying, the both of them. Sam knew it. Everyone in the uncomfortable little group knew it, but she couldn't blame them for wanting to get out of the line of fire though knowing Amanda, she was probably romanticizing the whole thing.

Demetrios's hand tightened on hers again. *Don't make a fuss,* he was telling her, but why would she? The things she had to say to him were best said without an audience, especially one made up of family.

Moments later, after hugs and kisses, handshakes and phony smiles, they were alone. Sam jerked her hand away and glared at Demetrios.

"I don't know what kind of game you're playing," she snapped, "but it won't get you anywhere."

"Such anger, Miss Brewster. Such hostility. Could it possibly be a disguise for your real feelings about what happened that night?"

"Nothing happened."

"Anger is a safer emotion than embarrassment."

Sam flushed. Maybe he was right, but she'd choke before she admitted it. "You mean, it's safer than bad judgment. If I hadn't had that *caparhinia*—"

"Imagine that. A reserved spinster with a drinking problem." Demetrios folded his arms. "Your brother-in-law would be fascinated to hear it."

"I don't have a problem. I was tired. And surely you don't expect me to believe Nick described me as a reserved spinster!"

"No. Certainly not. Rafe said that. Nicholas merely said that he had a sister-in-law who was an excellent translator." He smiled coldly. "I had no reason to think they were describing the woman who'd promised everything and delivered nothing that night in Brazil."

"Goodbye, Mr. Karas."

Demetrios took her elbow, deftly maneuvered her into the booth and slid in beside her.

"Your brothers-in-law see you as an intelligent, honorable woman leading a lonely existence. By the time they finished describing you, I pictured a stick in a tweed suit."

"I am intelligent and honorable," Sam said, wincing for having said something so nonsensical. "I am certainly not lonely. And if you think of women as stereotypes, that's your problem, not mine."

"I had to lie to Nicholas—to my good friend—to protect your, ah, honor."

"You lied to protect yourself, Mr. Karas. As for my honor, it's never been in question—not that it matters. This entire thing, starting with what happened at Rio de Ouro and ending with this supposed job offer, is best forgotten."

"This is not a 'supposed' job offer, Miss Brewster. I have need of a skilled linguist."

"Find one."

"I have found one. You."

"I'd sooner translate for Vlad the Impaler."

Demetrios smiled thinly. "I don't think he's been doing much hiring the past couple of centuries. On the other hand, now that I think about it, your credentials don't suit my needs."

"My credentials happen to be excellent," Sam said tightly.

"I'm sure you're a competent academic, Miss Brewster." Demetrios looked up, caught the waiter's eye and mimed lifting a cup to his lips. "But I have a complex business deal to handle. French, Italian, very colloquial but with lots of legal terms thrown in…" He shook his head. "No, it wouldn't work. The more I think about it, the more I doubt you could handle it."

"You doubt I could…" Sam's mouth flattened. "I suppose your opinion would change if I were wearing tweed?"

"It would change if you had not spent your professional life translating poems and love letters." The waiter appeared at the table with coffee. Demetrios paused, waited until they were alone again. "My needs are much more stringent. I need a translator who can judge the meaning behind a word, behind an intonation." He smiled politely, lifted his cup and drank. "Clearly, Miss Brewster, you lack the necessary qualifications."

"You have a distressing habit of leaping to conclusions, Mr. Karas. It just so happens my specialty is exactly the kind of translating you've just described."

"Really."

A little smile—smug, masculine, totally self-assured—accompanied the word. Sam gritted her teeth. How could she ever, *ever,* have found this man attractive? He was arrogant beyond belief, self-centered, conceited…

"What I cannot even begin to comprehend," she said coldly, "is why anyone who knows me would have thought I'd find you the least bit interesting."

Demetrios raised one dark eyebrow. "Did they?"

"So it would seem, which only goes to prove how foolish some people can be."

"Well, I can't comprehend why anyone who understands

the complexity of business would have thought I'd find you suitable as a translator.''

"What have you been doing for the past several months, Mr. Karas? Oh, don't bother answering. I know what you did.''

"Indeed.''

"You sat around counting the money you inherited from your father while I worked my tail off, keeping a bunch of prima donna ethnologists from killing each other over who'd made which discovery first in a Danian village in Anemaugi.''

"Anemaugi?''

"Indonesia. Borneo, to be specific. You'd have hated it. Mud huts, no running water, no electricity…'' Sam smiled coldly. "On the other hand, you might have found the economy right up your alley. It's based on pigs.''

His mouth twitched. "I take it there's not much call for your skill at translating poetry in—''

"Anemaugi. No,'' she said, wishing she *had* slugged him so he wouldn't be giving her that supercilious little smirk, "there isn't.''

"No love letters, either?'' He grinned at the look on her face. "Just asking, Miss Brewster.''

"No poems. No love letters. Just months of tough, brain-twisting work.''

"Excellent.'' Demetrios put down his coffee. "In that case, you're hired.''

"Are you deaf or just dumb? I wouldn't work for you if—''

"I would expect you to sign a four month contract.''

"I just said—''

"What did you earn for your job in this charming back-water?''

Sam knew the figure, precisely. Without a moment's hesitation, she doubled it, spat out the resultant number and waited for Demetrios to gape. He didn't.

"Per month?"

She almost laughed. "What do you mean, per month? Of course—"

"I'll double it."

He'd double it? Sam stared at him in disbelief. She'd been about to tell him that the outrageous sum she'd invented was what she'd been paid for the entire stint in Indonesia. Even halved to the true amount, it had been damned good money, more than she'd earned in the past. "Combat pay," the museum that hired her had dubbed it, for putting up with the ins and outs of academic warfare.

What Demetrios had just offered made that amount pale by comparison. Nobody would pay a translator so extravagantly, not unless translation was only part of the job description.

"That's too much," she said bluntly.

"I don't think so."

"Well, I do. I've been in this business for six years. People don't pay that for a translator."

"I've been in business twice that long and if I have learned nothing else, it's that you get what you pay for."

"And what, exactly, is it you think you'd be getting from me?"

Demetrios grinned. "Your very special ability, Miss Brewster. Your talent...with languages. What else would I expect to get for my money?"

"That's my question, Mr. Karas. What would you expect?"

"Your skill." His smile faded; his tone turned crisp. "This will be delicate, perhaps difficult, work. I would want to be informed of every nuance as you discern it, every possibility you suspect but cannot confirm. You would have to be available to me twenty-four hours a day, seven days a week." His expression hardened. "Do you think I am so in need of a woman to warm my bed that I would hire one, or lure her there with dollars? I assure you, that is not the case."

No. Sam suspected that it wasn't. Demetrios Karas wouldn't have to offer a woman anything but himself to get her into his bed…and that was just the problem. Hadn't he almost gotten her there within minutes of their meeting?

But she'd turned him down and regained her sanity. That surely counted for something. Besides, this was the opportunity of a lifetime. Not just the money, although the amount was staggering. It was the job itself that sounded irresistible. She loved language, loved nothing quite so much as searching for the hidden meanings in words…

"Well?"

Sam cleared her throat. "I'm willing to give your offer some thought. Give me your telephone number and I'll get back to you later this week."

"That will be too late." Demetrios pulled out his wallet, tossed a handful of bills on the table. "I'm afraid I need an immediate answer."

"How immediate?"

He looked at her, his eyes cool, his expression unreadable. "I leave for Greece in the morning."

"Then, I'll call you there."

"If you want the position, you will leave with me. If not…"

His shrug, a casual lift of those broad shoulders, said it all. She would either take what he'd offered or she'd turn it down. From the look of him, he didn't care which choice she made. This was business, as he'd claimed… Or was it?

"Yes or no?" he said brusquely.

Sam hesitated. Then she took a deep breath. Don't be an idiot, she was going to tell him…

Instead, she told him yes.

CHAPTER FOUR

BY EVENING the rain had ended, leaving the sky over Manhattan a surprisingly tender blue. A soft breeze, redolent of the newly budding trees in the little park behind Samantha's apartment, teased lightly at the curtains in her bedroom as she packed.

Packed? Sam looked at the open suitcase on her bed and the things inside it. Nobody could call some underwear, a couple of pairs of cotton slacks and a handful of T-shirts "packing," not if you were going to be out of the country for four months.

Four long, endless months.

She sighed, sank down on the edge of the mattress and leaned back on her elbows. She'd wasted the last few hours pacing her small apartment. Now time was running out, not just for packing but for deciding if she'd made a mistake in accepting Demetrios's challenge. That was what it had been; why pretend otherwise? Can you work beside me for all that time without tumbling into my bed? He hadn't said that, of course, but that was the message.

As for what else he'd said, about not having to buy women... Of course he didn't buy them. He didn't have to. Women took one look at Demetrios Karas and wanted him. *She'd* wanted him, Sam thought with disgust. Hadn't she almost slept with the man within minutes of first seeing him? Now, somehow, he'd maneuvered her into saying yes, she'd work for him, she'd go to Greece with him, spend days and nights at his side...

Maneuvered her into it? Sam got up, grabbed an armload of blouses from the closet and slung them onto the bed.

His "maneuvering" had been done with all the delicacy

of a waltzing elephant. The man had made her a job offer only an idiot would refuse. She knew there were people who assumed she didn't have to worry about supporting herself because she was Jonas Baron's stepdaughter. The truth was, Jonas would have gladly supplemented her income, if she simply asked, but Sam had always cherished her independence.

She made her own way in the world, the same as she never backed away from anything difficult, and so far, things had gone well. She was a long way from getting rich but she paid her bills. And she'd never done anything truly crazy, either, well, except for things like bungee jumping off a bridge in Australia or swimming with sharks off the Seven Sacred Pools in Maui...

And saying yes, she'd go to Greece with a stranger.

"Hell," she muttered, and grabbed for the phone. The only thing worse than making a bad decision was not admitting it. Yes, Demetrios had offered her a lot of money and yes, she certainly could use it, but she'd survived dry spells before.

It's Samantha Brewster, she'd say politely. *Something's come up, Mr. Karas. I'm afraid I'll have to forego your job offer.*

At least, she'd tell him that once she knew where to reach him.

Sam sat down, hit a speed-dial button, crossed her legs and swung her foot impatiently as Amanda's answering machine picked up.

We're sorry, her sister's voice said cheerfully, *but we can't take your call just—*

"Amanda? Amanda, can you hear me? I know you're there. And this is as much your fault as anybody's. Pick up the—"

"Sam? What's the matter?"

"Nothing. Everything." Sam took a deep breath. There really wasn't any point in letting out her anger on her sister. She was the one who'd accepted the job offer, not Amanda.

"Do you know how to reach Demetrios Karas? Is he at a hotel, or does he have an apartment in the city?"

"Well—"

"Because I need to talk to him, and he very conveniently didn't give me his number."

"Well—"

Sam's good intentions flew out the window. "Dammit, will you stop saying that?"

"Well—I mean, why are you so upset?"

"Why do you meddle in my life?"

"Don't answer one question with another," Amanda said primly. "Besides, I don't meddle."

"You do. You almost stood on your head to get me to meet this—this Greek God."

"I take it," Amanda said, muffling a snort of laughter, "that you're referring to Demetrios."

"Yes, Demetrios. Unless you know some other man who thinks he's the walking, talking reincarnation of—of Adonis."

A gusty sigh came over the phone line. "I thought you liked him."

"What gave you that impression? His cockeyed story, about how he insulted me at Carin's party?"

"Well, yes. I mean, that's what happened, isn't it? You met, he was called away, you got annoyed and you left."

"Do you honestly think I'm that self-centered?" Sam said, before she could think.

"Well…" Amanda cleared her throat. "Sorry. Uh, no. I don't think you're self-centered at all. Actually—actually, I have to admit, I had the feeling there was more to it than that. I even said so to Nick, and Nick said, well, maybe there was, because he'd seen Demetrios later that same evening…" Her words trailed to silence.

"And?" Sam said sharply. "What did Nick tell you?" Had her brother-in-law seen through the afternoon's charade? Had he figured out that she was the woman in the stable with Demetrios?

"Nothing. That was all of it. Nick sort of broke off in the middle of a sentence and changed the subject."

Sam felt a sudden pounding in her temple. She walked into the bathroom, yanked open the medicine cabinet and took out a bottle of aspirin.

"Sam?"

"Mmm?"

"You haven't answered my question. Was there more to it than Demetrios told us at lunch? Did something happen that night at Carin's?"

"No."

"Come on, sis. Remember when we were kids? I could always tell when you were lying."

Sam jammed the portable phone between her ear and her shoulder, opened the bottle and dumped two aspirin into her palm, then into her mouth. She made a face, added one more tablet for good measure, and swallowed hard.

"Yeah, but we're not kids anymore."

"It doesn't matter. I can still tell. You and Demetrios *did* meet that night, didn't you? The story wasn't quite as simple as he made it sound."

Wearily, Sam sank down on the edge of the tub. There was no sense fighting both her sister's instincts and the crazed musician who'd set up his drums inside her skull.

"All right. We met. And yes, something happened. To be specific, something almost happened. But it didn't. And before you ask, no, I am not going into details."

"Wow."

"Wow? What kind of response is that? I tell you something happened—something almost happened—and all you can say is, 'wow'?"

"That's so romantic. It's like Nick and me."

"How can you say that? You don't know what went on. And, trust me, it was nothing like you and Nicholas. I mean, you told me the story. How you met through his sister. How you and he agreed on a business arrangement, that you would redecorate his penthouse and that, over a period of time, the relationship changed, went from businesslike to something more personal...Amanda?'' Sam's eyes narrowed. Her sister was not given to deafening silences, but one was humming between their telephones right now. ''That's what happened with you and Nick, isn't it?''

Amanda cleared her throat. ''Not exactly. Things were, um, they were a little more volatile.''

''Volatile.'' Sam's eyebrows lifted. ''As in, you didn't hit it off right away?''

''Uh-huh.''

''There's more, isn't there? I can tell.''

''Honestly, Sam, this has nothing in the world to do with you and Demetrios.''

Sam gave a weary sigh. ''Maybe not. Look, I'm supposed to fly to Greece with him tomorrow. And I can't seem to decide if I should or shouldn't do it.''

''You're leaving the country?'' Amanda's voice rose. ''With Demetrios?''

''He lives in Greece,'' Sam said, her tone dry. ''His business interests are in Greece. Where did you think I'd be working, Mandy? In Brooklyn?''

''Yes, but Greece... I mean, to go so far away with a man you hardly know...''

''Don't tell me you're starting to be sorry you pushed Demetrios Karas under my nose.''

Amanda sighed. ''I didn't push. I'm just surprised you'll be leaving so quickly.''

''That makes two of us.''

''But there's nothing to worry about. Neither Nick nor I would introduce you to anybody who wasn't a decent, honorable person.''

Honorable, Sam thought. Decent. Oh, yes. Those were certainly adjectives she'd use to describe a man who'd tried to get into her pants without even knowing her name. Not that he'd had to do much to convince her. Not that she hadn't been a more than willing participant.

"Sam?" Amanda's voice softened. "Please. Tell me what's wrong."

"Nothing. Not really. It's just—it's just that I..." Sam hesitated. "If you didn't like a man, if you found him irritating, arrogant and altogether a pain in the rear but he offered you a terrific job, would you take it?"

Silence, broken only by the soft sound of Amanda's breathing. Then, finally, an uncomfortable murmur. "I, uh, I might."

"Suppose—suppose on top of all that, you were, uh, you were attracted to him? I mean, you disliked him but there was—there was this something, this—this feeling—"

"Is that the situation between you and Demetrios?"

Now the silence was on Samantha's end of the line. After what seemed a very long time, she sighed. "I don't go for men like him. For one thing, he's far too sure of himself."

"Authoritarian," Amanda said. "I know the type."

"Exactly. Authoritarian, demanding, and used to taking charge. And I do not want to be taken charge of, Mandy. That's not my style at all."

"But there's this—this appeal..."

"Maybe. In some, uh, some very basic way."

"I know."

"You do?"

"You asked how it was with Nick and me when we met. Well, it was like that. The initial antipathy. The fast sizzle." Amanda's voice held a smile. "And then we fell in love and got married."

Sam shut her eyes and rubbed her forehead. Her sister had marriage on the brain.

"Mandy," she said gently, "believe me, this has nothing to do with love and marriage. I am not the least bit interested in love and marriage. Neither is Demetrios. This has to do with sex."

"Sex is part of love."

"For you," Sam said gently. She stood up, walked back into her bedroom and looked at the open suitcase still lying on her bed. "It isn't, for me. I don't sleep around. You know that. But I don't think going to bed with a guy has to lead to the altar, either. There have been men in my life, Amanda. Nice men. Great guys, some of them. But I'm never foolish enough to equate lust with love. I think it's terrific that it works for you and for Carin, but that doesn't mean it's what I'm looking for."

"In that case, you've answered your own question. Why worry about going to Greece with Demetrios? If you end up having an affair with him, you'll enjoy it. And if you don't, well, then you've lost nothing. Right?"

Sam thought it over. It was such a logical equation. Why hadn't she come to it on her own?

"Right," she said, after a few seconds. "Definitely right. But you have to promise me, no more meddling ever again. I don't want you fixing me up. Or trying to fix me up."

"Okay," Amanda said, far too quickly.

"I'm serious. Don't say 'okay' when what you really mean is that you'll wait a couple of months and do the same thing all over again. You understand me?"

"Samantha—"

"Swear! Like when we were little."

A sigh came over the phone. "'Cross my heart, hope to die, honest and true, it's not a lie.' Are you satisfied? Look, if you don't want to settle down, if you don't see falling in love, getting married and starting a family as something you—"

Sam groaned. "You're never going to stop, are you?"

"Oh, come on! I just said I would. And, you know, now that I think about it, I already did. Stop, I mean. If I were playing matchmaker, why would I have thought it was a terrific idea for Nick to tell Demetrios what a great translator you were?"

"So you could get the two of us together, any way possible," Sam said sweetly.

Amanda chuckled. "Okay. Maybe. But," she said, turning serious, "this is a real job. Nick says it's going to need skill. He says that Demetrios made it very clear he wouldn't hire you just because you're my sister."

"That was before he knew I wasn't just your sister, I was the woman he'd almost—" Sam caught her lip between her teeth. "It was before he knew who I was."

"That's my point. He didn't know who you were, just that you were a great translator. That was why he wanted to meet you."

Sam sighed. "Yeah, yeah, yeah."

"Honestly, you're making this more complicated than it has to... Jason? Jason, stop that right now! Give back your sister's teething ring. Jason, you are four years old, you're a big boy, and... Sam. Honey, your nephew just stole the baby's toy. I'll have to cut this short. I can call you later. Well, no. I can't do that. We're going out to dinner. Look, I'll call you in the morning. First thing."

"I won't be here. I'll be on a plane, to Greece. That is, I'm supposed to be on a plane, to Greece."

"You sure about this?"

"No. Oh, not because of what might happen between Demetrios and me. I mean, what you said is right. If something did happen, if we got involved... But we won't. In fact, after this afternoon, I can't even figure out why I thought I was interested in him at all. He's everything I dislike in a man. Controlling. Overbearing, self-centered, disgustingly macho and too damned good-looking to be let loose."

"Yum, yum."

Sam couldn't help it; she laughed. Amanda laughed, too, then cleared her throat.

"Sis?"

"Yeah?"

"I know what you just said. I know what *I* said...but do me a favor and watch yourself, okay? I guess I'm ready to admit that you're not looking for Mr. Right, but that doesn't mean your heart can't be broken."

"My heart isn't the part of my anatomy the Greek God

wants," Sam said dryly. "And all I want from him is the money he's promised for my services. It's going to be business, nothing else."

"That's what they all say."

"Yes, and some of them—me, for example—actually mean it." Sam winced as a baby's sobs and a little boy's shrieks rose to a deafening pitch. "Kiss the kids for me," she shouted, "and don't worry. I'm a big girl. I can take care of myself."

"You sure? Because if you're not—"

"I'm positive. I'll call you from Greece."

She would, Sam thought, as she put down the phone, unless she changed her mind about going. That was still her privilege.

By ten, she'd finished packing. She scrubbed her face, brushed her teeth and got into bed wearing cotton panties and an oversize T-shirt she'd bought at a flea market in Paris for no better reason than that she liked the parade of poodles high-kicking across its front. It was late and she was tired, and if she woke up with doubts, she thought as she set her alarm clock, she could always meet the irritating Mr. Karas in the lobby and tell him what he could do with his job.

Satisfied, Sam punched her pillow into submission and fell asleep.

By ten, Demetrios was still pacing the floor of the bedroom in his New York penthouse, high above Fifth Avenue.

He was not in a good mood, a fact he'd made abundantly clear hours earlier to his cook when she'd asked if he was ready for dinner, and to his houseman, who'd committed the unpardonable sin of smiling when he greeted him.

Demetrios had snarled at the both of them. Once inside his bedroom, he'd shed his jacket, undone his tie, opened the top buttons of his shirt and rolled up his sleeves. Then he'd caught a glimpse of his face in the mirror, sighed, picked up the intercom and made apologies, however brief, first to the cook and then to the houseman.

Why let his anger out on them, when the person who'd caused it was Samantha Brewster?

But his temper didn't cool down, not even when he tried diverting it by dictating some notes into a small digital recorder.

"Memo to my broker," he said, as he paced the bedroom. "If the market share on Invixa slips again, you are to contact me immediately, before…"

Before what? How could he concentrate on business when he was still trying to figure out why in hell he'd hired Samantha Brewster for a job she probably couldn't do, despite all Nick's hype? A woman could be beautiful and still be intelligent. He was not foolish enough to think the combination impossible. But this woman went beyond beautiful. She was like a cat: sleek, soft and elegant, purring and stretching under a man's hand as if she desired his touch before suddenly turning into a spitting demon that was all teeth and claws.

She was a tigress, and he had just arranged to spend four months with her at his side

Demetrios groaned, tossed the recorder on the bed and stalked to the window. What in hell had possessed him to employ her? It was a ridiculous question. He knew the answer. Lust. Lust had possessed him, and at his age, with his experience of women, admitting to such a thing was disgraceful.

He'd listened to his hormones instead of his head and hired a woman who could not, would not be able to do the kind of subtle translations he needed. And even if, by some miracle, it turned out that she could, did he really want her around as a temptation?

"No," he growled.

Hell, no. He did not. He had not come this far in life by acting on impulse, by doing things that were rash. He studied companies before he invested in them, ideas before he let himself believe in them. He hired only the best people, and never before seeing their references.

Until now.

All he'd done was mention his need for a highly competent linguist to Nick. And Nick said, well, as it happened, he knew just such a person. She was his sister-in-law. Yes, one of Amanda's sisters.

Demetrios had nodded, but he hadn't been impressed. First Amanda had a sister who couldn't find her own man; now, she had one with a degree—a post-graduate degree, Nick had emphasized—in an amazing number of languages. It seemed too much to swallow but Nick was his friend so he'd said, well, wasn't that interesting? And when Nick asked if he'd like to meet her, what could he have said but yes?

What he'd meant was that he'd meet with her as a courtesy. And if, by some miracle, she seemed competent, he'd made it clear that he was promising nothing except to have her credentials vetted. There was no rush. He had translators back home that he'd used before. It was only that he suspected they were too academic, too literal for situations in which inference might be just as important as accuracy.

Demetrios put his palms against the cool window glass and stared down at the city lights twinkling far below him.

All those intentions had vanished when he'd discovered that Nick's supposedly brilliant sister-in-law was the very woman he'd almost made love to that night in Brazil, discovered, as well, that she was as beautiful in the flesh as she'd been in his memory all these weeks.

One look at Samantha and all his plans and logic had flown out the window. He'd ended up offering her much more money than he'd intended—much more than she'd expected, judging by the look on her face. And if that weren't enough, just to be sure she took the bait, he'd framed his job offer as a challenge, the kind he knew, instinctively, she would not be able to turn down.

Demetrios shook his head.

So much for the conventions by which he lived. He'd grown up in a household in which the regulations were legion; he had not made the mistake of repeating that pattern of rigidity but he did have a few immutable rules by which he lived.

He never did anything carelessly. He didn't behave precipitously. And he never mixed business with pleasure.

So, what had he done this afternoon? Broken every one of those rules, that was what. He was flying to Greece with a woman who might not speak French or Italian any more fluently than he did, a woman he'd almost taken to bed, a woman who could still stir his passion even now, after she'd walked out on him, made a fool of him, treated him as if he were dirt.

Had he lost his mind? His own stupidity enraged him…but there was a solution. You had to know when to cut your losses.

This, most assuredly, was the time.

Demetrios grabbed his suit jacket, dug through the pockets. Nick had given him Samantha's address and phone number. He'd pulled out the slip of paper when he put her into the taxi. What had he done with it after that?

There it was, in his breast pocket. He glanced at it, crossed the room, started to pick up the phone…and saw the time. Midnight. Was he really going to phone at this hour and tell her he'd changed his mind about employing her? No, he was not. She might read something into it, might assume there was some urgency in his need to call off their deal.

Besides, it would be far more pleasurable to give her the news in person.

He would go to Samantha's apartment in the morning, as planned. He'd wait in the lobby and when she appeared, he'd be polite, soften the blow with a check that was the equivalent of a month's pay and say that he'd thought things over and changed his mind. If she insisted on a reason, he'd tell her that he really wasn't sure she had the skills necessary for the job.

Yes, he thought, with a little smile of contentment. His

smile broadened as he undressed. It was good to feel back in command again. That was where a man should always be, where a woman was concerned.

Still smiling, definitely satisfied, he got ready for bed, punched his pillow into submission, and fell soundly asleep.

He awoke at six, well before the buzz of his alarm.

He shaved, showered, dressed. The penthouse lay draped in early morning darkness when Demetrios tossed his carry-on bag into the back seat of the black Ferrari he kept in the garage beneath the building. He drove through quiet city streets. It was a Sunday, when New Yorkers slept in.

Samantha's apartment building was shabby, its saving grace the tiny pocket park behind it. He frowned as he parked his car. No wonder his job offer had brought such a shocked expression to her face. Clearly, she needed the money, but her finances were not his problem.

He trotted up the steps to the front door. At least it was locked, he thought grimly... No. It wasn't. The knob turned easily and he stepped into a small lobby. A woman should not live alone in such insecure circumstances—but that was not his concern, either.

Demetrios glanced at his watch. He was a few minutes early. He shifted from foot to foot. It was almost as cold inside the lobby as it was in the street...if you were foolish enough to call this miniscule space a lobby.

He looked at his watch again, then at the mailboxes lining the wall to his left. *S. Brewster, Apartment 401*. At least she had the presence of mind not to list her entire name and let the world know that she was a woman who lived alone.

She did live alone, didn't she?

Not that that was his affair, either.

Dammit, a man could get claustrophobia trapped in a space hardly larger than a telephone booth, breathing in air that was redolent of cabbage. He glanced at the staircase ahead and sighed. Four flights to climb, he thought, and started up. Was that how she kept that beautiful body trim?

His frown deepened.

He hadn't come here to think about Samantha's body or how she lived her life. He'd come to tell her, in person, that their deal was off, and to give her the check he'd tucked into his pocket.

Her apartment was at the top of the stairs. He took a breath, cleared his throat, ran a hand through his hair…

"Hell," he muttered, and stabbed the doorbell with his finger.

Nothing happened. He scowled, glanced at his watch. She was supposed to meet him downstairs in a few minutes. Wasn't she up? Wasn't she dressed? What kind of competency did such behavior suggest?

Not much, he thought coldly. It was a good thing he'd decided not to hire her.

He rang the bell. Rang it again. And again. And…

The door opened a crack, stopped by the length of a security chain. He could see half of her face as she peered out at him. An eye. A cheek. A tumble of wet, curling, autumn-dark hair.

"You," she said tightly.

"Me," Demetrios said, just as tightly. "Open the door, Miss Brewster."

"Why? What are you doing here? You're not due here for another twenty minutes."

"Ten minutes. Will you please open this door?"

Sam hesitated. What did he want? She'd just come out of the shower. She wasn't dressed for a confrontation with Demetrios. She knew how this would go. She'd tell him she'd decided against the job. He'd try to talk her out of the decision. It would be better to hold the discussion under more formal circumstances.

"Miss Brewster." His voice was sharp and commanding. "I am not in the habit of discussing business in tenement hallways."

Sam glowered at him. "This is not a tenement, Mr. Karas, but I suppose someone born with a 24-karat spoon in his mouth thinks any place without hot and cold running servants is a tenement.''

She shut the door, undid the chain, then flung the door open. What did it matter if she was wearing a terry-cloth robe she'd owned since college? If her feet were bare, her hair dripping onto the carpet, her face free of makeup? She didn't have to look like something out of *Vogue* to tell Demetrios to take his job and shove it.

"Very well,'' she said, her tone the equal of his, "come in.''

He stepped inside and wasted no time. "You're fired,'' he said curtly.

Sam folded her arms. "You can't fire me.''

"I can do whatever I choose, and I choose to fire you.''

"Not if I've already quit.''

He stared at her. "What do you mean, you've already quit? You can't do that!''

"But I have. I don't want to work for you.''

He hadn't expected that. Sam could tell because the scowl on his face turned to consternation. Lovely, she thought with delight. Had anyone ever walked out on the Greek God? She doubted it. Not an employee, if he paid them as well as he'd intended to pay her. Not a woman. What woman would turn away from him if he wanted her?

I would, she told herself, and lifted her chin.

"I see,'' he said. "You live in a place like this, and you turn down a job that pays as well as the one I've offered you?''

"A place like what?'' Sam glared at him. "This is how real people live, Mr. Karas, but I guess you wouldn't know that.''

"This building has no lock on the outside door. That security chain you hide behind could be taken out by one determined push…''

What was he doing? How she lived, where she lived, was none of his business. Hadn't he reminded himself of that just a little while ago?

"Unless," he said softly, "you don't live alone."

Sam narrowed her eyes. "Thank you for your concern, but I don't need it or your money. I repeat, Mr. Karas. I quit."

Demetrios took a step towards her. Despite herself, she stepped back. The look on his face was frightening.

"And you think that will solve the difficulty between us? That all you have to do is run away and everything will be fine?"

"There is nothing between us. And I am not running away."

His eyes grew hot and dark. He moved closer; she stumbled back.

"You run, even now," he said softly. His gaze moved over her, down the length of her body, then up again. "What are you afraid of, Samantha?"

"Nothing," she said quickly, and hated how defensive she sounded. She'd had this all planned, and now... "I'm not afraid of anything. I just don't think working for you is a good idea."

"You lie."

She blinked. "Excuse me?"

He reached out. She jerked back, but not quickly enough. His fingers threaded lightly through her hair.

"Don't—don't do that."

"Do what?" His gaze moved over her face; she could almost feel it, like a caress. "Nicholas says you've done many things that take courage."

"Nicholas talks too much."

"He says you see life as a challenge." His hand slid to the nape of her neck and she fought the almost overpowering desire to close her eyes and purr under his touch. "And yet, you fear me."

Sam jerked free of his hand. "That's ridiculous!"

"You fear what it would be like to find yourself in my bed."

"My God, what an ego you have!"

"Is it because you know how it would be between us? That you'd lose all control in my arms?"

"All right. That's it." She brushed past him, reached for the door. "Goodbye, Mr. Karas."

Demetrios caught her wrist. "I would be a lover who demands your soul as well as your body," he said in a rough whisper. "That terrifies you."

She was trembling and she didn't know the reason. Nothing he said was true. She wasn't a wide-eyed innocent, afraid to lose her virginity, afraid she would find such a transcendent experience in his arms that it would leave her empty once their affair ended.

She was trembling with anger, that was all. Anger, at his incredible conceit.

"You'd like to think that," she said, "but my reasons for not wanting to work for you are much simpler. I don't want to work with a man who wants to seduce me. I don't believe in sleeping with my employer. My career depends on my reputation, and it's far too important for me to jeopardize it."

"Fine."

"It took me a long time to establish my credentials. People who deal with me know that I'm all business."

Demetrios nodded. "Very well."

"I'm not about to do anything to... What do you mean, 'very well'?"

"I mean that you're right. I, too, keep the two parts of my life—business and pleasure—separate from each other."

Sam stared at him. "But—but a minute ago, you were—"

"I accept your terms, Samantha."

"What terms? I didn't—"

"We'll shun all intimacy and maintain a working relationship only. Do you agree?"

She blinked. In the past five minutes, she'd quit, he'd fired her, he'd told her that sex with him would turn her world upside down but that sex would be off limits. Was she crazy, or was he?

"Are you saying you've decided not to fire me?"

Hell. That was what he was saying, all right, and how had that happened, when his very first words to her had been, "You're fired"?

"Yes," he said calmly, "I have."

"Why?" Sam folded her arms. "What changed your mind?"

The sight of you, Demetrios thought, *the look of challenge in your eyes, the scent of your skin, the softness of it...*

"It's a business decision. I admit, I was...irritated."

"Irritated? By what?"

"Miss Brewster. Samantha. Must we—"

"Yes. We must. And I much prefer Miss Brewster, Mr. Karas."

Demetrios gritted his teeth. "Very well, *Miss* Brewster. It was your attitude."

"*My* attitude? Oh, that's wonderful. That's incredible." Her eyes flashed with anger. "I do not have an attitude, Mr. Karas. You, on the other hand, have nothing but."

"Then we are more than a match for each other. Unless..."

"Yes?"

An insolent smile angled across his mouth. "Unless you don't think you're up to the challenge."

"My God!" Sam threw up her hands in disgust. "Your conceit is appalling."

"Is that a yes?"

"Yes," she snapped, "it most certainly is."

"Fine." He took a step towards her, caught the ends of her belt in his hands. "In that case," he said softly, "I have only two more questions."

Sam's heart lifted into her throat. He was drawing her towards him, undoing the sash. Stop him, she told herself, don't let him do this...

His eyes locked on hers as he parted the robe. "Are you naked under this robe, Miss Brewster?"

The hoarsely whispered question stunned her. Slap him,

she told herself, put your hands on his chest and push him away.

Instead, she lifted them, curled her fingers into his shirt. Her body was on fire and Demetrios hadn't even touched her—but he did, now. He slipped his hands beneath the robe, slid them up her back, then down, stroked her as she tried not to tremble.

"And are you a good translator?"

She caught her breath as he cupped her naked bottom, lifted her to him, brought her against his erection, and she felt a silken wetness bloom between her thighs.

"No," she said shakily, "I'm not good. I'm excellent."

He gave a soft laugh, lowered his face, bit lightly at her throat. "Fine. Because that's all I want of you, *gataki*. Do you understand?"

"What did that—" Her breath hitched. His hands were moving on her, sliding over her skin. "What does that mean? What you called me?"

"Kitten." He cupped her breasts, stroked his thumbs over her nipples, and she made a sound that was almost a moan. It was all he could do not to lift her in his arms, carry her to the sofa and take her, bury himself inside her. "Are we agreed, then? You will work for me. Nothing more."

The idea wasn't even a possibility. How could it be, when just his touch was driving her insane? "Samantha?"

But she had never walked away from a challenge. She was strong, not weak. Why walk away when all she had to do was find the right balance of power?

"Yes," she said, "we're agreed." Slowly, she ran the tip of her tongue over her bottom lip, then rose on her toes. "But I want you to know what you'll be missing," she whispered, and she put her hands in his dark, silky hair, drew his head down to hers and lost herself, if only for a moment, in the heat, the passion, of his kiss.

CHAPTER FIVE

IT WAS raining in Piraeus, the seaport that had been Athens' commercial lifeline to the world for more than 2500 years.

Rain was unusual in the Greek islands at this time of year, especially a downpour like this. Demetrios, seated at the head of an olive-wood table in the conference room of Karas Lines, watched as the fat drops beat against the windows. The effect was hypnotic. That was what he told himself each time his attention wandered from the meeting.

It was safer to pretend he was diverted by the rain than to admit he couldn't concentrate because of Samantha. Samantha, who had burned in his arms that morning in New York—and who had since turned into an Ice Queen.

She was seated to the left and slightly behind him, the very essence of efficiency and decorum. He couldn't see her, not without turning around, but he knew exactly how she looked. It was the same, day after day, week after week. By now, her image was lodged in his brain. She sat straight, holding a notepad and pen in her lap. Her knees were carefully aligned, her ankles demurely crossed. If she moved, it was only to write something on the pad or, occasionally, to lean towards him and speak softly into his ear.

That was what she'd done a few moments ago and he hadn't heard much of what anyone said since then. His senses were still on overload, trying to get past the almost imperceptible brush of her breast against his arm, the scent of her skin.

It would have been easier to stop breathing.

How could a man drive such things from his mind?

Hiring her had been a mistake. Not because she wasn't good at what she did. On the contrary. When he'd asked her if she was good, she'd said she wasn't just good, she was excellent. It was true. She was the best translator he'd ever employed.

She was also the only one who had ever made it impossible for him to keep his mind on business. No one had ever had that effect on him before.

Did she know? How could a woman who never smiled at him, who never offered a word that was not related to her job, manage to find ways to drive him crazy?

She'd just made a notation—his senses were so attuned to her that he could hear the faint scratch of pen on paper. The Italian seated across from him, a man who owned a long-dead title as well as a company that built the fastest, most elegant cruise ships in the world, was droning on and on, mostly in English though he occasionally lapsed into his own tongue and turned to his translator for help. Demetrios was doing his best to pay attention but for the life of him, he couldn't have repeated a single word the man had just said.

He could, however, describe Samantha's perfume. Vanilla. Jasmine. Something delicate. Mysterious. She'd just leaned towards him again and murmured something in his ear. The faintest drift of her fragrance carried to his nostrils but he felt the impact in a far different part of his body.

"Excuse me," he said abruptly.

He pushed back his chair, smiled—or hoped he smiled—and gave a casual wave of his hand to indicate that everyone should continue talking. His secretary had laid coffee and pastries on a table near the windows and he strolled to it, carefully examined the tiny cakes as if his life depended on making the correct selection even though the thought of biting into one and actually trying to chew and swallow it was beyond the realm of possibility.

Instead, he poured a cup of coffee he didn't want. It gave him an excuse to stay away from the conference table and his unsmiling, silent, stiff-necked translator, the woman he'd agreed not to view as a woman...and how in hell could he manage that, when just the whisper of her nylons each time she crossed or uncrossed her legs was an aphrodisiac?

His reaction was ridiculous. He knew it. Determinedly, he turned his back to the conference table, lifted the coffee cup and sipped at the hot liquid.

A man wasn't supposed to think the things he was thinking when he was in the middle of a multimillion dollar business deal. He wasn't supposed to sizzle with tightly controlled anger, either. You needed a cool head when you dealt with people like these.

No sex.

He and Samantha had made an agreement, and he was adhering to it. Why wasn't she?

She was a walking, talking, breathing symbol of seduction, and never mind that look of cool removal, the stark black suit and low-heeled shoes, the way she drew all that incredible hair away from her face and clasped it, demurely, at her neck.

Demetrios's hand tightened on the cup.

He should have fired her that morning in New York. To this moment, he couldn't figure out what had happened. All he knew was that things had gone wrong somewhere between that dingy lobby and her tiny excuse for an apartment. Not only had he veered from his original intention, he'd lost the upper hand.

One moment Samantha had been telling him she would not work for him, and the next... The next, he'd touched her. Felt the heat of her skin, the silk of her breasts. Tasted the sweetness of her mouth. And then she'd kissed him, all but given herself to him in that kiss...

God. He couldn't do this. Have these thoughts. Let these memories turn his body hard and hot with desire.

All of this, *all* of it, was her fault. Why had she kissed him that morning? To tease him? To drive him out of his mind and leave him wondering what it would be like to take her to bed? But those moments had affected her, too. He could still hear her soft moans, feel the race of her pulse beneath his lips. He knew when a woman was lost in the heat of passion, and she had been lost that morning in his arms.

Could she forget that easily?

Anger hummed in his blood. Evidently, she could. Otherwise, she would not treat him as if he were a stranger. He swung around and looked at her. And she would not behave like this, smiling across the table at the Frenchman who owned a company the equal of the Italian's and laughing at something he said.

A cold knot formed in Demetrios's belly. Where were her ethics? Surely, she knew better. She worked for him. He had the right to expect her loyalty and obedience. Did she think she was here to socialize with the men with whom he did business?

Why didn't she do what was expected of her? Nothing had gone as he'd intended. Not here. Not at his home on Astra, where he'd instructed his housekeeper to prepare a guest suite for her. Samantha had changed his plans in the blink of an eye.

"What's that?" she'd said as his helicopter set down on his private island.

He'd barely glanced at the small house in the garden. "A guest cottage, but hardly anyone uses it."

"I'll use it," she'd said. "That will give me the space and privacy I need to set up my computer and printer."

"There is plenty of space in the main house," he'd replied, and immediately found himself in the unbelievable position of arguing with an employee who didn't seem to understand that it was her place to accept his decisions without question. That he'd let himself be drawn into such a situation still made him furious.

"Stay where you wish," he'd said coldly, and ended the dispute.

She had.

She lived in the guest house, took her meals there despite his logical protestations.

"You are to dine with me," he'd said, striding through the door to her quarters that first night after he'd found his dining room table set for one and listened to his housekeeper's halting explanation of how the *Amerikanίoa* had told the gardener, who had told the laundress, who had told her, that she would take her meals on a tray in the guest house.

Demetrios had clenched his fists. "She told the gardener, who told the maid, who told you?"

Yes, the housekeeper said. The gardener spoke a little English, because he had a daughter who lived in America. The laundress, who had once lived in America, was more proficient, so the gardener asked the laundress to speak with the *Amerikanίoa*, and she said it was true, she would eat alone, and she would come to the kitchen to collect her own tray and to return it.

"To the kitchen," Demetrios had ground out, between his teeth. "How thoughtful of her."

He'd gone directly to the guest house and walked in, unannounced, to tell her she would learn to do as she was told, but Samantha had other ideas.

"In the future," she'd told him, "please remember to knock and wait to be admitted."

"Admitted?" he'd said incredulously, "admitted to my own guest house?"

"As long as I'm living in it, yes. As for dining with you…" She'd smiled politely. "You pay me to translate for you, Mr. Karas. That service does not include dining with you."

What answer could he have given to such a statement? She saw dining with him as an obligation? So be it. He'd only been trying to be kind to her, a stranger in his country, but he was glad she'd turned him down. Why would he want to look across the table and see her each evening? It was far better to dine alone.

But, yes, he paid her to translate for him. That meant he expected her beside him all day, every day, at the office.

She didn't seem to understand that. For a week, he'd watched her hurry out of the building whenever they broke for lunch, then watched her return with her cheeks pink and glowing, her hair just a little disheveled.

She had a lover, he'd thought, and before the rage inside him had completely taken over, he'd realized that was ridiculous. Samantha knew no one in Piraeus or, for that matter, in Athens. Apparently, she took her lunch alone. The others—the Frenchman, the Italian, even their translators— often joined him for lunch in his corporate dining room. It was a small but handsome room, and there was a café not far away that could be counted on to send over whatever was requested.

The others seemed more than willing to avail themselves of the arrangement. Why didn't she?

In the second week, he'd asked his secretary, very casually, if she knew where his translator went each day during lunch.

"She walks," his secretary said.

"She walks? Here? Alone, on the docks?"

His secretary had shrugged as if to agree that such a thing was unheard of. "Yes, sir. I suggested it was unwise, but—"

"But, she does not take advice," Demetrios said grimly, and his secretary had nodded.

He'd waited for Samantha to return. Then he'd explained that it was not safe for a woman to wander this part of Piraeus alone. He'd done it quietly, carefully, so that she might understand his concern was not the least bit personal but was only for her welfare, which was his responsibility.

It would have been more sensible to have expected a pig to fly.

"My welfare is *my* responsibility, thank you."

Only a fool would not have known the simple words were meant as an insult. He was certain she would have gone right on with her midday strolls but, like it or no, she *was* his responsibility. She was a foreigner working in his country, for him. So, the next morning, he'd announced that he had given the matter some thought and he'd decided it would be more efficient…"and more conducive to our reaching an accord," he'd added with a hard-won smile…if they had lunch as a group not just occasionally but as a daily practice.

From then on, they all met for a catered meal in the corporate dining room—until today, when Samantha had gone to lunch with the Frenchman.

"You don't mind if I steal *Mlle.* Brewster for an hour, do you, *mon ami?*" the Frenchman had said over morning coffee.

Mind? Demetrios thought, *mind?*

There was a soft peal of feminine laughter behind him. He turned around. Samantha had left her chair. She was standing with the Italian. And with the Frenchman. The damned Frenchman, who'd breezed off with her at lunchtime as if she did not have a first, hell, a sole obligation to the man who was her employer…

"Miss Brewster," Demetrios said. "Perhaps you would like to tell me what it is that you find so amusing?"

The room fell silent. He'd meant to sound lighthearted, as if he wanted to join in the fun, but from the way everyone was looking at him he knew he hadn't pulled it off. Carefully, deliberately, he drew his lips back from his teeth.

"I hate to miss a good joke."

No. Definitely not. He hadn't fooled anybody. The Frenchman cleared his throat. "It was nothing, Demetrios. I merely asked your charming Miss Brewster a question in English and she explained that I had misused a phrase and thus given my question an entirely different meaning. Isn't that right, *mademoiselle?*"

"Oh, but your English is generally excellent, *monsieur.*"

Sam's voice was warm and low-pitched. She never speaks to me that way, Demetrios thought. She never looked at him that way, either, with a little smile. She never looked at him at all.

"You are too kind," the Frenchman said pleasantly, "but I know that my English leaves something to be desired."

It was the man himself who left something to be desired, Demetrios thought coldly. He had a translator of his own. Why did he need to talk to Samantha at all? And even if he did, she didn't have to reply.

He would tell her that, later. Miss Brewster, he would say, from now on, you are to speak only to me...

Demetrios took a deep breath. *Thee mou,* he thought, I am losing my mind!

He was deep in negotiations it had taken months to set up, verging on a deal that was worth a huge sum of money. More than that, he was about to take his company in a direction he'd dreamed of for years. He should have been hanging on every word that was uttered in this room, but he wasn't. He couldn't. His concentration was close to non-existent.

The rain, he thought desperately, it had to be the rain.

Sam returned to her place at the conference table and sat down. He followed and told himself to forget everything but the meeting. The Italian began speaking. Demetrios could catch the meaning of some of the words but, of course, he would rely on his translator's expertise. He turned towards her. He'd learned to watch her face as she listened, to read her expression for subtle changes.

She was leaning forward, her brilliant emerald eyes fixed on the Italian as if he were the only man who'd ever interested her. Why didn't she ever look at him that way?

Because she's not trying to translate your words, his brain told him calmly.

His battered ego wasn't listening.

How could she do that? Smile at one man, go to lunch with another, and treat the one who employed her as if he didn't exist.

Because, his brain said patiently, *that's what she's paid to do.* That was her job; it was what they'd agreed, that morning in her apartment. He was pleased because she'd turned out to be an excellent translator. So what if she was also a beautiful woman? The world was filled with beautiful women. This one was nothing special. She was nothing to him at all. Hadn't he proved that by never referring to what had almost happened in Brazil? By not letting her absence at his dinner table annoy him?

How could it annoy him, when he hardly ever spent the evening at home?

He sent her back to Astra in his helicopter each night. He stayed in Athens, dining out, getting home late, knowing she had to hear the roar of the 'copter as it made the return trip...not that she ever mentioned it. She didn't give a damn what he did or who he did it with, not that he was doing anything but eating dinner in his club and then burying his nose in the day's papers because his friends and acquaintances had taken to avoiding him.

"Trouble with a woman?" one had asked him the other night, and he knew he'd damn near snarled when he said no, why would he have trouble with a woman? Especially with this one, who he didn't want despite a face that surely would have put Helen of Troy to shame and a body Aphrodite would have envied.

"...not quite what it seems," Samantha whispered, her breath warm against his ear.

Demetrios snapped back to reality.

She was leaning towards him, speaking softly as if they were lovers lying in each other's arms. It was only an illusion. She spoke of dollars and gross tonnage, not of passion and heat, and her language was formal, Mr. Karas this, Mr. Karas that, and the occasional "sir," which she always managed to make sound like an insult.

Did she think addressing him as Mr. Karas would make him forget he'd almost taken her to bed the very first night they'd met?

His vision blurred. He held his breath, reminded himself that he was not the least bit angry—and exploded.

"A sto dialolo!" he growled, and shot to his feet so quickly that his chair fell over.

The silence beat against his eardrums. They were all staring at him, as if he'd changed into a dangerous animal.

Maybe he had.

He bent down, picked up the chair and righted it. Then he faced the little assemblage.

"My apologies," he said stiffly. "I seem to—to have developed a sudden headache."

He waited, but no one spoke.

"I suggest we adjourn for the day. We've made progress." They'd made none, but what was the harm of one more lie? "But it is getting late." That was true enough. It was dark outside. "And the rain will make the roads slick." Another bit of truth, if not a vital one. "So, what I suggest…" What? What did he suggest, that would erase the bewildered expressions from the faces turned towards him? "What I suggest, since this is Friday, is that we meet tomorrow morning at, say, nine o'clock at my home. My driver will be at your hotel at eight. He will take you to the airport, where my helicopter will be waiting." He managed to smile. "Perhaps we can discuss some of our concerns more easily in a less formal setting."

Chairs were pushed back. Hands were shaken. Coats were put on, umbrellas gathered. People hurried to the door. Demetrios followed after them…and clamped a hand on Samantha's shoulder before she could leave.

"You will stay."

The look she gave him would have turned any normal man to stone but he was not a normal man. Not right now. He was a man filled with an anger he didn't fully understand and that only helped convince him that his rage was her fault.

"I beg your pardon?"

"I said, you are to stay."

"Am I really?" Her eyes flashed. "Perhaps you'd like to amend that to an order to heel, sit and stay."

Demetrios shot a look past her. "Lower your voice," he growled.

"I am not a dog in need of training." Her voice quivered with anger. "I do not sit or stay or do anything else on command, and I have nothing further to say to you. Good night, Mr. Karas."

"You will not speak to me like that!"

"And you," she said, shaking off his hand, "will not embarrass me in front of anyone, ever again!"

The look on his face was wonderful. Anger? Disbelief? No. Better than that. It was shock. Sam figured that nobody had ever told off the Greek God, nobody had ever dared to, not in his entire life.

"Goodbye, Mr. Karas," she said, and strode away.

"Come back here," he shouted.

Sam quickened her pace. She heard him pounding after her, then heard the murmur of his secretary's voice and his harsh response, but his footsteps stopped.

"Samantha? Samantha! You will wait for me!"

Like hell she would. She burst from the building, waved away Demetrios's driver, ran up the street, took the corner at top speed and didn't slow down until she'd taken another half dozen turns. Then she slowed to a walk while her breath made steamy plumes in the chill darkness and an icy, wind-driven rain beat into her face.

She paused to get her bearings. Where was she? She'd walked these fascinating, ancient streets until Demetrios had put a stop to it, but never at night. Well, it didn't matter. Nothing mattered except seeing to it that she never saw Demetrios Karas again.

How dare he? How *dare* he speak to her that way?

You will stay.

Sam shivered and pulled up her collar.

The no-good, self-centered, domineering son of a bitch! Ignoring her, day after day, except when it suited him to boss her around. Announcing she would take her meals with him, as if he owned her. Forcing her to have lunch in his company for no good reason. All that nonsense about her being his responsibility...

She'd never been any man's responsibility. She never would. Her mother had gone that route and look where it had taken her. First she'd been a doormat for a weak man; now, she was the possession of a powerful one. Her stepfather treated Marta like a cherished piece of crystal kept safe on a shelf. And yes, Amanda and Carin were headed for that same kind of existence.

Sam quickened her steps.

No, thank you. Not only wasn't she interested in marriage, she wasn't interested in getting involved, even temporarily, with a man who thought of women as responsibilities. That was just a polite way men had of saying they had the right to dictate what women did with their lives.

Demetrios wasn't her husband, he wasn't her lover, he wasn't anything but her boss and he'd already tried caging her. He'd tried to install her inside his house; he'd put a stop to her going off on her own at lunchtime. He wanted to watch her every move.

Did he actually think she'd let him do that? Treat her as if she were his property, except for the times he treated her as if she were invisible? Nothing but a grunt when she boarded his stupid helicopter each morning. Another grunt at night. Not that they returned to his island together all that often. He was too busy at night in Athens, doing whatever it was he did with whomever he did it. His secretary, maybe, and never mind all that stuff about not mixing business with pleasure.

The woman looked at him as if he was the most desirable man on the planet.

He wasn't.

He was a walking ego. A self-important ruler of his own little kingdom. He was a man who thought he was irresistible to women.

Well, he wasn't. Not to her.

Sam burrowed deeper into her coat and bent her head against the wind.

She'd seen right through him from day one. It was a damned good thing she hadn't fallen into the trap and gone to bed with him. The nerve of him, to speak to her as he had just now. To look at her the way he'd been looking at her all afternoon, as if he'd finally remembered she was a woman, as if he were weighing the possibility of throwing everybody out, locking the door, backing her into a corner and doing things…

Hot, delicious things.

Sam shuddered again. She didn't want any of that. Not from him.

A horn blared as she stepped off the curb. A car flew past and she jumped back but not in time to prevent a wall of cold, dirty water from drenching her from head to foot. She glared after the car and muttered a phrase that described exactly what she thought of the driver in the Greek she'd learned on the streets.

Mr. I-Am-The-Law Karas would have been surprised at how much Greek she'd picked up since she'd come here. She listened; she learned. That was what linguists did. Now she knew lots of polite words—and lots of impolite idioms. That had been one benefit of those lunchtime walks, until Demetrios had decided to leash her. So she'd known what to call the idiot driver who'd just soaked her to the bone.

More to the point, she knew what Demetrios said just before he'd overturned his chair.

A sto dialolo, he'd snarled. To hell with it.

If he meant, to hell with their arrangement, she agreed. Completely. She had no business here. Saying she'd work for him had been stupid. She should have stuck to Plan A, told him to take his job and stuff it, just as she'd intended.

Dammit, the puddles were ankle deep. There had to be a taxi around here. If only she knew where she was but everything looked different at night. Everything felt different, too.

The back of her neck prickled and she picked up her pace.

No, she didn't belong here, not just in Piraeus but in Greece. She should never have let Demetrios turn his job offer into a challenge. Even that kiss...

Okay. So the kiss hadn't been his idea, it had been hers. And it had been stupid, just as it had been stupid to let him touch her, but the temptation to give him a taste of what he'd never have, had been too strong to ignore. He'd deserved that little lesson. He was too sure of himself, accustomed to taking what he wanted though, dammit, there was something incredibly sexy about all that macho ego...

And that was crazy.

Hadn't she always made it a point to avoid men who thought they owned the world and all the women who inhabited it? Hadn't she always known what such a man would be like as a lover? That he'd be dominating, and possessive, and jealous?

And incredible.

Sam's pulse beat quickened. She couldn't forget that morning, when he'd put his hands under her robe as if he had the right to do whatever he wanted to her. With her. It was wrong. The way he'd made her feel was wrong, but she'd relived the moment a hundred times. A thousand times. All she had to do was close her eyes and she felt him touching her, the sensual roughness of his fingertips, the drugging heat of his hands and his mouth...

A horn screamed into the silence of the night as she stepped off the curb. Not again, she thought...

Tires shrieked as they clawed for purchase on the rain-darkened road. Sam looked up, blinded by headlights. A car was bearing down on her. She cried out, stumbled back. The car fishtailed, spun; she tripped over the cobblestones.

The car came to a stop just as she sank down, shaking, on the curb.

A door slammed. Footsteps pounded towards her. A dark shape bent over her and hard, angry hands closed on her shoulders. A stream of Greek words blistered her ears.

She had almost killed herself, the man was saying.

Sam looked up. His face was masked in shadow. *"Seenghnómi,"* she whispered, "I'm sorry…"

It wasn't enough. She could feel the heat coming off him, the unbridled male fury. His hands tightened on her and he drew her to her feet.

A different kind of fear kicked in, a fear born not of her brush with death but of this enraged stranger.

"No," she said, struggling against him. "Don't! I'll scream!"

"Scream all you like," Demetrios said grimly, and he swept her into his arms, carried her to his car, and dumped her inside.

CHAPTER SIX

DRIVING a car, especially one with four hundred and eighty-something horses under the hood damned near begging you to let them run free on the twisted streets of an ancient city, was not a good idea when your gut was churning with anger.

Demetrios knew that. He also knew that it was better to let out his emotions this way than to pull to the curb, turn to Samantha and confront her. She had done something so stupid that it had nearly cost her life. No, it would not be wise to stop the car. If he did, he'd shake her until her teeth rattled...

Or pull her into his arms and unleash his bottled-up rage in a kiss that would make it clear she'd had no right to run away from him, that he would not permit her to do such a thing again.

At least he could still think clearly enough to know that taking either action would be a mistake, so he slammed the car into gear and stepped hard on the gas.

"I could have run you over," he said as they sped through the darkness. She didn't answer. That only made him angry enough to drive a little faster. "What did you think you were doing, huh? Stepping off that curb without so much as looking? Did you think you were in a jungle in Borneo?" He drew a deep, ragged breath. "You should not have been walking these streets to begin with. I told you they were not safe, told you and told you..." He clamped his lips together, tightened his hands on the wheel, fought for self-control. "Are you all right?"

She was soaked. She was shivering. And her ankle hurt. "Yes," she lied, "I'm fine."

"Anything could have happened to you. Why did you do something so foolish? Why did you run away?"

"You wanted to argue. I didn't."

"I did not want to argue," he said grimly. "I wanted to talk to you, that's all."

"We had nothing to talk about."

Nothing to talk about? She'd spent the day flirting with another man and they had nothing to talk about? Demetrios's jaw tightened.

"I am your employer. If I wish to discuss something with you, I will do so."

Hell. He sounded like an idiot. Samantha had to think so, too, but she said nothing. That only egged him on.

"Do you hear me? Do you understand what I'm telling you? If I wish to talk to you, if I wish you to remain behind after the others leave…" He paused, frowned. "What did you say?"

"Nothing."

But she had said something in a papery whisper. An apology? She'd done that already—had she really offered it in Greek? At least, he thought coldly, she understood how close she'd come to being seriously hurt.

Samantha, hurt.

A hand fastened around his heart. He considered pulling over, taking her in his arms, telling her that she'd had no right to scare him…

"It's too late to show contrition," he said coldly.

Only the purr of the engine and the rumble of the tires on the cobbled streets broke the silence.

"What you did was stupid."

Still, she remained silent. His frown became a scowl. Why didn't she respond? Was she just going to let him call her stupid, give her orders? No. That wasn't Samantha.

Something was wrong. For the first time, he looked at her. *Thee mou!* His mouth went dry. She was huddled in her seat, head back, eyes shut. He could hear the labored hiss of her breath.

"Samantha?" She didn't answer, and he pulled to the curb. "What's wrong?"

She shook her head. "Nothing."

"Don't lie to me," he said roughly, as he reached for her. "Are you hurt?"

She didn't answer. He put his hand under her chin, made her look at him. Light from a car coming towards them played across her and he cursed sharply. Of course she was hurt! Her eyes were enormous. Her face was colorless, except for a bruise on her cheek and another on her temple.

No, he thought, no...

"Panagia mou," he whispered, and enfolded her in his arms. "What have I done to you, *gataki?"*

"It was my fault."

"No, sweetheart." He stroked her wet hair. "I shouldn't have been driving so fast, but when I stepped out of the office and Andreas told me you had run off..."

"Exactly. It was stupid. And then I—I stepped off the curb without looking..."

Worse and worse. She was bruised, probably in pain, and she was contrite. That was almost more frightening than anything else. He cupped her shoulders, drew back so he could look into her eyes, then gently touched her temple.

"Does this hurt?"

"No." A shudder went through her; the sound of her breathing grew ragged. "It's my ankle. When I jumped back...I must have landed wrong. My ankle made this—this funny sort of pop."

Demetrios's stomach tightened. He twisted in his seat, tried to see her feet, but there wasn't enough space.

"Can you move your foot, *gataki?"*

Sam nodded. "Yes. But it hurts."

Quickly, he got out of the car, went around to her door and opened it. He took a flashlight from the glove compartment, squatted down and tried to see her ankle.

"Dammit," he muttered. "I can't..."

What was he doing? She said her ankle hurt. What good

would it do him to look at it? What she needed was a doctor. And fast, he thought helplessly, because now she was trembling. From the cold? From shock? God, what had he done to her?

Demetrios peeled off his jacket and carefully folded it around Sam's shoulders, waiting for her to object, to argue, to tell him what he could do with his jacket and his concern…but she burrowed deep into its warmth.

"Better?"

"Y-yes."

"Good."

But it wasn't good. She should have been sniping at him, accusing him of being an idiot; she should have batted away his hands when he buttoned her inside the jacket. Her quiet passivity terrified him.

"You'll be fine," he told her.

She nodded.

"Fine," he said again, in a voice that would brook no disagreement. Then he clasped her shoulders gently in his hands, bent to her, pressed the softest of kisses on her trembling mouth and told himself that ankles were, after all, only ankles…

But this was Sam and the realization that she was in pain, that he had caused it, was almost more than he could handle.

There was a hospital only blocks away.

Was it best to drive fast, and get her there quickly, or to drive slowly to be sure he didn't jar her by hitting bumps or potholes in the road? Compromise seemed the best solution. He drove at a speed that was half what he normally did and twice the crawl he'd considered.

Sam's teeth chattered; in between, she made muffled sounds of distress. She was hurting, his invulnerable, unshakeable tigress. Please, he thought, please, let her be all right.

Time slowed, seemed to stop, but finally he reached the hospital. He parked in front, ignoring the signs that warned against it. Carefully, so carefully, he lifted her into his arms. She made a little sound and he crooned soft words of comfort as he carried her into the building, words he had not heard since the earliest, almost forgotten years of childhood—words he had never used before.

There was no one in the waiting area. Demetrios strode to the reception desk. "We need a physician," he said.

The woman behind the desk looked up. He saw boredom in her eyes as she looked at him, then at Samantha.

"What is the problem?"

"This woman is hurt."

"That's what I asked you. What is the problem?"

Demetrios told himself to stay calm. It would help nothing to explode.

"She fell."

"Fell where?"

"On the street."

"What street?"

He felt his jaw tighten. "It was dark. I did not look for street signs. What does it matter? I tell you, she is hurt."

The woman took a form from a drawer. "I will need her name and address."

"Her name is Samantha Brewster. She lives with me."

The woman looked up. "And where is that?"

He told her. He told her whatever she asked while time, and his patience, waned. Sam shifted in his arms, gave a soft hiss of pain. He thought about putting her in a chair, then vaulting the counter, grabbing the clerk and shaking her.

"And how did this fall take place?"

"Miss Brewster stepped in front of my car. I blew my horn, tried to stop. She was startled and she jumped back."

"A vehicular accident. I see. Have the police been notified?"

"It was not a vehicular accident!"

"But you just said—"

"I didn't hit her with the car."

"I distinctly understood you to say—"

"Demetrios," Sam said faintly, "make sure she understands it wasn't your fault."

"She speaks English?"

"She is an American."

"Ah. In that case, there are two other forms that—"

"The forms can wait." Again, Demetrios told himself to stay calm. Anger would not help; he had dealt with enough officious clerks in enough countries to know that. "She needs a doctor immediately. She is hurt. Something is wrong with her ankle. And she is shaking. For all I know, she is in shock."

"The forms—"

"To hell with the forms," he roared. "Send for a doctor!"

"Sir. You cannot give orders to me. I must have this information. Some of these papers require the lady's signature. After that, you will wait until you hear your name called. Do you understand?"

"Perhaps *you* should understand what your superiors will do when they learn that a man who sits on the board of directors of this hospital was kept waiting."

The clerk blanched. "What did you say your name was?"

"I am Demetrios Karas. And I wish to see a physician—an orthopedist—at once."

"Of course, sir. If you would be so kind as to take a seat, I'll call for the doctor immediately."

He took a seat, held Sam close in his arms, warmed her with his body. She said something too softly for him to hear and he bent his head towards her.

"What, *gataki?*"

"I said, that was quite a..." Her teeth chattered. "...a p-p-performance. Are you r-r-really one of the hospital's directors?"

"Who knows?" He smiled. "It is possible. I donate to many charities and sit on many boards. It is difficult to keep track."

"Almost as difficult as it is to k-k-keep track of your ac-accent."

"What accent? I have no accent."

Sam almost laughed. "You sound different, when you're upset."

"Different?"

"Yes. Very old world. Very Greek."

"I had not noticed," he said, and winced because he knew she was right. "We will add that to your job description," he said gently. "From now on, you will not only translate for me, you will tell me when I begin to sound too old world."

"You never sound—" Sam caught her breath. "You never s-sound too old world. And I'm quitting my j-job."

"You cannot quit," he said calmly. "We have a contract."

"We d-don't. We nev-never signed anything."

"We have a verbal agreement. Such agreements are contracts. Would you try and break a contract with a man powerful enough to intimidate a civil service tyrant?"

Their eyes met. Hers were still dark with pain; her face was still pale. Was that a grimace on her lips or was she trying to smile?

"Sir?"

Demetrios looked up. "Yes?"

"The doctor will see you now."

"An orthopedist," he said as he rose to his feet with Sam in his arms.

"The head of orthopedics," the clerk said, and as Samantha buried her face in Demetrios's neck, he definitely felt her lips turn up in a smile.

The bruises on Sam's face were nothing.

Bruises would not have shown up so quickly, the doctor explained. These were simply smudges of dirt and the nurse who attended the orthopedist and anticipated his every need carefully sponged them away with cotton dipped in alcohol.

The doctor checked Sam's pupils and assured Demetrios they were fine. So was her coordination. She wasn't in shock, either. She was cold from the night and the rain.

The nurse shooed him out of the examining room long enough to take off Sam's soaked clothing and wrap her in a hospital nightgown, a hospital robe, and a blanket.

When he stepped back into the cubicle, his heart ached at the sight of her. His fierce kitten looked more like something the cat had dragged in. He kissed her forehead, sat in the chair beside her and clasped her hand while the doctor examined her ankle. He was very gentle but Sam clenched her teeth, then cried out with pain.

Demetrios almost went wild. "You are hurting her!"

"I am trying my best not to do so, Mr. Karas."

Sam let out a strangled gasp. Her nails dug into his palm.

"Dammit," Demetrios said, "you must be more careful."

The doctor looked at him. "You have a choice, Mr. Karas," he said softly. "You may stay here and be quiet or you may go out to the waiting room until I am done. Which will it be?"

Demetrios wanted to argue. He wanted to tell the man who had wrenched that cry from Samantha that he took orders from no one, that if he dared hurt the woman clutching his hand like a lifeline he would—he would...

"Please, Demetrios," Sam whispered. "Don't make a fuss."

The pleading words took the fight out of him. "I won't let them send me away." He brought her uninjured hand to his mouth. "I will behave," he said humbly. "I promise."

Somehow, he managed to keep his word, even when it took a moment longer to get her to the X-ray lab than he thought it should, even when they wouldn't let him go inside with her no matter how he argued. By the time the doctor reappeared, Demetrios was pacing the corridor.

"Well?" he said impatiently, "how is she?"

"Would you like to join me for some coffee, Mr. Karas? It has been a long day and a longer evening, and—"

Demetrios grabbed the orthopedist's arm. "Just tell me what happened to her, dammit!"

The doctor sighed. "Miss Brewster sprained her ankle. It's somewhere between a grade one and a grade two sprain."

"What does that mean?"

"It means she's probably torn a ligament. It's painful and it will take a bit of time to heal."

"It isn't a fracture?"

"No, no, the ankle's not broken. Actually, she's fortunate. Even a severe sprain can sometimes require surgery."

Demetrios closed his eyes. He remembered his anger at knowing Samantha had set off alone in the dark, rain-washed streets, anger that had changed to panic when she'd suddenly stepped into the path of his car.

"It's all my fault," he said, swallowing hard. "She stepped off the curb. It was raining, and I was driving too fast…"

The doctor nodded. "She will be fine," he said gently.

"I want the best surgeons," Demetrios said. "And a second opinion. No offense, Doctor, but before you operate—"

"No one will operate," the doctor said, even more gently. "As I said, Miss Brewster was fortunate. Her injury is painful, not dangerous. She'll need to keep the ankle strapped for a few days and I've given her something for the sprain. She will be fine."

Demetrios stared at him. "Is that all?"

"Absolutely. My assistant is putting an elastic bandage on the ankle." He clapped Demetrios on the back. "Your lady is fine, Mr. Karas."

"She works for me," Demetrios said quickly, "that is all. And I am much relieved at what you've told me, Doctor."

"I'm happy to hear it. Now, if you don't mind, I'm going home before my wife no longer recognizes my face."

"Yes. Of course." Demetrios smiled and held out his hand. "How can I thank you?"

"You might see to it that the board considers another residency program so that we're not so overworked here."

"Consider it done."

"Just do yourself and the patient a favor, will you? Calm down before you drive her home."

"I can take her home tonight?"

"Unless you'd rather she spent the night in the hospital."

"I will take her home," Demetrios said firmly. The shiver of pleasure that went through him at those words was something he preferred not to dwell on.

They gave him a vial of little tablets and instructions to give Sam one every four hours if she was in pain.

She wasn't in pain now. Whatever they'd already given her was working. Demetrios could see it in the loopy smile she gave him. She was still wrapped in the hospital gown, robe and blanket. The nurse handed him a plastic bag that contained Sam's soaked clothes and assured him that there was no hurry to return the borrowed things.

"Up we go," Demetrios said softly, and lifted her into his arms again.

Sam curled her arms around his neck, sighed and lay her head against his shoulder.

"Wher're we going?"

Her words were slurred. Her breath was warm. *She* was warm, and he thought how amazing it was that she should feel so right, in his embrace.

"Home, *gataki,*" he said softly, as he carried her to his car.

"Mmm," she said thickly. "Home."

"Yes, *mátya mou.* Home."

He strapped her into the seat beside him, drove to the helipad as carefully as if his precious cargo were made of glass. She was sound asleep when he carried her onto his helicopter and she was still asleep when he carried her into his house—a house she had never seen, except for the kitchen.

His usually unflappable housekeeper looked shocked when she saw him. "Oh, my goodness," she said. "What happened, sir?"

"Miss Brewster hurt her ankle," he said softly, even though he suspected it would take a herd of stampeding Cape buffalo to rouse the woman nestled in his arms. "She will need care for the next few days."

"Certainly, sir. Perhaps you want to put her in the Blue suite. If you wish, I can put a cot near the bed and sleep there so that I'll be nearby if she needs me."

"Yes, thank you, Cosimia. That might be…" He stopped in midsentence. "On second thought, it won't be necessary. Miss Brewster will stay with me."

His housekeeper's mouth dropped open. "With you, sir?"

"Yes," he said calmly, as if the idea were the logical outgrowth of a careful thought process, "with me. It will be simpler that way," he added briskly. "I can use the sofa in my dressing room, if you would be good enough to make it up."

He sat in an armchair near the window in his bedroom, the warm burden that was Sam in his arms, while Cosimia did as he'd asked.

Sam, he thought, smiling a little as he looked at the pale, perfect face, the slightly parted lips, the mass of autumn hair that had come loose of its clasp and dried in a frill of wild curls. Such an incongruous name for a woman so feminine, so beautiful—and yet, the name suited her spirit. Her tenacity.

She had claws, his kitten, and she was never afraid to use them.

"All done, sir," Cosimia said softly.

"If you would just turn down the blankets on my bed…"

"I've already done that, sir."

"Thank you."

The door snicked shut. Demetrios didn't move for a long time. At last he rose and carried Sam to his bed. She opened her eyes as he eased her down gently against the pillows.

"D'metrios?"

He smiled. "Hello."

"What're we doin'?"

"Getting you to bed, *gataki*," he said softly. He put his arm around her, held her against him as he slid the bulky hospital robe from her shoulders. "Does your ankle bother you?"

Sam frowned and peered at her leg. "Whatsat?"

"What...? Ah. It's an elastic bandage."

"Waffo?"

It took a few seconds to decode. "What for?"

"Mmm."

"You hurt your ankle. You had an accident."

"Uh-huh. I'member. Dark street. Rainy. Stepped in front of car." Sam blinked. "Yourcar," she said, making the two words one.

"My car," he said tightly. "Yes." He laid her back against the pillows, still wearing the hospital gown. Sam's eyes closed.

"Stilldress."

Stilldress? He shook his head. "I don't understand, sweetheart. What is 'stilldress'?"

"Me," she murmured, and tugged at the gown. "Stilldress."

Of course. She was still dressed, still in her underthings. Could he let her sleep in them? Or—or...

His throat constricted. He knew what to do. Ring for Cosimia. Ask her to come to his room, to undress Sam and slip her into something cool and silken. But even as he thought it, he was undoing the ties of the hospital gown, sliding the gown off her shoulders, letting it fall to her waist, fumbling at the closure of her bra.

Demetrios caught his breath at her beauty, at the small, rounded lushness of her breasts and the elegant contrast of colors: the pale gold of her skin, the deep apricot of her nipples. How smooth her shoulders were, under his hands...

He dropped the robe to the carpet, tortured himself with a quick glance at the strip of lace between her thighs, then laid her down against the pillows.

"Umm. Nice," she whispered, her eyes still tightly closed.

"Very nice," he whispered back, and drew up the silk duvet.

She sighed, let out a long breath. He waited until her breathing become slow and steady. Then he kissed her forehead, her eyelids, her slightly parted lips.

Briskly, he undressed and put on a pair of sweat pants in deference to his guest. He turned off all the lights but one that he dimmed, went into his dressing room, left the door open so he could hear Sam should she need him and lay down on the sofa. It was too short for his long legs but he was exhausted and he groaned with pleasure at the cool caress of the sheets. He shut his eyes, rolled over, rolled over again...

Sleep evaded him. He kept listening for Sam; kept getting up, going into the bedroom, standing over her to make sure she was all right.

Sometime during the endless hours of the endless night, he heard her moaning. "Sweetheart?" he said, and he threw back the blankets and hurried to her side. She was sitting up, the duvet clutched to her chin, still groggy enough to stare at him blankly.

"Demetrios?"

"Yes." He sat down beside her, stroked a tangle of curls from her forehead. "Do you hurt, *gataki?*"

"My ankle feels like an elephant's sitting on it."

Quickly, he brought her one of the tablets the doctor had given him, poured her a glass of cold water.

"Open your mouth," he said softly, holding his hand to her lips.

She took the tablet, her tongue brushing lightly over his

palm. A shudder went through him and he cursed himself for being an animal. Only an animal would feel desire now, when she was hurting.

"That's good. Now drink some water."

She took a sip, sighed and sank back against the pillows. He watched her for a moment before bending to her and brushing a gentle kiss over her mouth.

"Sleep well, kitten," he whispered.

"Stay with me," she sighed against his lips.

"Sam. Sam, you're—you're as good as drunk…"

"Stay," she said softly, and looped her arms around his neck.

"I cannot," Demetrios said. "Sweetheart—"

She was asleep, still holding him, still with her breath sighing from her mouth to his. He stared at her for what seemed forever. Then he drew her arms from his neck, pulled back the duvet and got into bed beside her. She sighed, turned into his open arms and he gathered her close, careful not to touch her injured ankle, careful not to let his body betray him.

This is torture, he thought. It was worse. It was hell. He would get no sleep this night, but he would see to it that Samantha was safe. He would hold her, protect her, soothe her if she awakened again…

Demetrios sighed, closed his eyes, slipped his fingers under Sam's silky hair and cupped the back of her head. She sighed, too, and snuggled against his shoulder.

It was the last thing he remembered before he fell into a deep, deep sleep.

CHAPTER SEVEN

HER ankle hurt.

Sam moaned, then bit her lip against a whisper of pain.

It really, really hurt, though maybe not as bad as when she was seven and Billy Riley said she was a girl and girls didn't have the guts to swing out on the rope over the Nautuck River, and she'd said he was too dumb to know anything about girls—except that her hands slipped and she'd ended up coming down in the shallows, coming down hard. And when Dr. Carter asked how she'd managed to break her leg, she said it was all Billy Riley's fault and that she was gonna beat him up as soon as the cast came off.

Then the doctor gave her some medicine and she'd floated away. Just closed her eyes and floated.

"Sam? Can you hear me, sweetheart?"

"Mmm." That was nice. Dr. Carter had his arm around her. It felt good.

"Sam?"

"Uh-huh." She sighed. "I'm floating," she said happily.

"Yes, kitten. I know. Does your ankle still hurt?"

Sam gave a giant yawn. "Uh-huh."

"The ice will help bring down the swelling. I'm sorry I can't give you anything more for the pain. You've had a reaction to the codeine...Sam?"

Ice. Ice on her ankle. Heat everyplace else. She was warm. Nice and warm and...

"Snugly."

"Good. That's my girl. Just lie back against my shoulder."

Nice shoulder. Hard and comforting. Sam frowned. How

99

come Dr. Carter smelled so good? He always smelled of mothballs and something her mom called Old Spice...

"Sam?"

She didn't remember Dr. Carter's voice being like that, either. So low. Husky. Sort of—sort of sexy.

"Can you open your eyes?"

Why would she want to do that? She felt fine. Snugly. "Issit still night?"

"Yes, sweetheart. It is."

She sighed, burrowed against the doctor and fell asleep to the feel of his stubbled cheek brushing gently against hers.

She slept, drifted, awoke again. A voice murmured in her ear.

"Sam? Are you awake?"

"Mmm."

"Does your ankle hurt?"

Did it? No. She shook her head, burrowed closer. "Thirsty," she whispered.

"Sit up, then. Just a little. Fine. Good. Now, take little sips."

She drank. The water was cool. Wonderful, going down her throat. Darkness had given way to the gray light of early morning but she didn't want to get up. Not yet.

"Doan wanna wake up yet," she sighed.

"No. You go on sleeping, *gataki*. Here, lie—Sam? What are you doing?"

But he knew what she was doing, turning in his arms so that they lay a breath apart, putting her arms around his neck, giving him the faintest, sweetest of smiles.

"Demetrios?"

He nodded, afraid to speak.

"Demetrios," she whispered, "you're not Dr. Carter."

He wanted to laugh but he didn't trust himself. "Who, sweetheart?"

"Dr. Carter. Mothballs. Liver spots. Ol' Spice."

"No," he said solemnly, "that isn't me."

"I know." She touched his face, let her hand linger against his cheek. "I'm glad."

Demetrios took her hand from his face, kissed the palm and curled her fingers over the kiss. He wasn't Dr. Carter, whoever that was. Neither was he a saint. Perhaps the best thing would be to go back to the sofa in the dressing room. A decent man would do so. A moral man...

"You're Demetrios," she murmured. "And you smell good."

He groaned. His body was hard as stone. "Sam." He curled his hand around her wrist, tried to draw back and put a little distance between them. "Sweetheart, now that you feel better, I'm going to—"

Her mouth, her sweet, soft mouth found his. He hesitated, then gave in to what was happening and kissed her.

"Sam." Once again, he thought of how wrong that sweet nickname had seemed, and of how right it now felt on his lips. It was a soft, lovely name, just like her kiss. It belonged to her just as she belonged to him. As she would belong to him. "Sweetheart? Do you know what you're doing?"

His question was answered by a gentle snore. Demetrios smiled. His beautiful Sam, his sweetly drunken Sam, had fallen asleep at the worst possible moment—or maybe at the best. Sighing, he gathered her close. Would she remember any of this tomorrow? Would she hate him? Would she want him? And, if she didn't remember, what was he going to do about it?

She threw her uninjured leg across his.

Demetrios could feel the sweat bead on his forehead. He counted to ten in Greek, in English, in every language he knew. Then, carefully, stealthily, he eased Sam onto her back, brushed his mouth over hers, rose from the bed and tiptoed from the room.

Sam opened her eyes.

The room was filled with sunlight. She was thirsty, her

head ached, and her ankle felt as if someone had used it for
an anvil.

Of course. The rain. The curb. The hospital. And then,
what? She frowned. Everything after that was a blank. She
couldn't dredge up so much as an image.

Well, maybe a couple. Demetrios, carrying her to his car.
Demetrios, carrying her into his house. There was more,
something hovering just around the edges of her mind.
Something about the night. The night, and this bed. And a
warm, hard body pressed against hers.

What kind of crazy dreams had she had? And what was
she doing in this room? She sat up against the pillows, ran
her fingers through her tangled curls, felt the soft breeze
from the partly opened window on her naked skin.

Naked? She never slept naked. She always wore something. A T-shirt. A cotton nightgown, but all she had on
now were her panties.

Sam grabbed the duvet, drew it to her throat. Then she
pushed it down and looked at her ankle. No cast, just an
elastic bandage. Good. It wasn't broken. Probably just a
little sprain, she thought, as she swung her legs to the
floor...

"Ah!"

Pain knifed through the joint the second she put weight
on her foot. She'd had sprains before. Were they supposed
to hurt this much? She thought back to the last time she'd
gone sky diving. Some guy had landed wrong. No break,
just a bad sprain, but he'd had to stay off his ankle for days.

Yes, but she couldn't just lie here and wait for somebody
to come along and tell her what the prognosis was. Why
was she in this room? Why was she half naked? How was
she supposed to get around?

Why did she keep thinking about a hard, warm body
pressed to hers?

If only she could remember something. Anything. Something beyond the rain. The car. The hospital. Demetrios,
carrying her. To his car. To this bedroom. To this bed.

"Kaliméra sas."

Sam yanked the duvet to her chin again and swung towards the door. "Oh." She gave a little laugh, told both her heart and her imagination to calm down. "Good morning, Cosimia."

The housekeeper smiled. They'd reached a kind of language accommodation over the weeks, a brew made up of the few words of Greek Sam knew, the few words of English Cosimia had acquired, and a lot of body language. It probably sounded and looked weird, but it worked.

Cosimia lifted her eyebrows, jerked her head towards the bathroom. *"Banyío,* yes?"

"I wish the *banyío,* definitely. But first..." How did you say 'naked'? "Um, I need something to put on, Cosimia. A robe. Something."

Cosimia raised her eyebrows. Sam mimed wrapping herself in the duvet.

"Clothes?" she said.

"Ah." The housekeeper nodded, made motions with her hands. Evidently, her things were being washed.

"In that case, I hate to ask, but could you go to the guest cottage? Bring me a sweat suit? Jeans? Shorts and a T-shirt?" Nothing. Sam sighed in resignation and mimed slipping her arms into a garment and tying it at her waist. "How about a robe?"

"Robe," Cosimia said, and beamed. She went to the closet and took out a navy blue robe. Sam smiled her thanks as she put it on. There was a pair of white terry-cloth robes in the guest cottage. Was she in a guest suite? Was the robe for the convenience of...

No. Sam froze. Then she lifted the collar and brought it to her nose. This robe belonged to Demetrios. It carried a musky scent mixed with the tang of the sea that she'd come to associate with these islands. It was his smell, and slipping into the robe was like going into his arms.

His arms, holding her through the long night.

"Banyío," Cosimia said politely, "yes?"

Sam blinked. "Yes, please," she said, and concentrated on leaning on the housekeeper's shoulder while she hopped to the bathroom.

Bathing, washing her hair, then drying it took time. Cosimia fussed; Sam asked questions but unless they were about soap and shampoo and toothpaste, she got no answers. Cosimia's English and her Greek couldn't seem to cover the night just past. The housekeeper shrugged her shoulders until, finally, Sam gave up.

"Okay," she said, while Cosimia brushed her hair as she sat on a vanity stool, "never mind. What I need now is a cane. A cane," she said, looking up. "You know..." She curled her hand over an imaginary handle and tapped the equally imaginary tip of a cane against the tile floor. "A cane, so I can go downstairs."

"Ah." Cosimia shook her head. "You stay, please."

An entire sentence, more or less, but not one Sam wished to hear. "I don't want to stay here," she said patiently.

"Mr. Karas—"

"Yes. I know. But Mr. Karas doesn't make rules for me, Cosimia."

"He say—"

"Never mind," Sam said, through her teeth. "House arrest," she mumbled, as she hobbled back to bed with Cosimia's help.

"*Kahfeh,* yes?"

"Yes. If you're sure I'm permitted coffee. I mean, shouldn't you check with Mr. Karas?"

Cosimia looked blank. Sam sighed and grasped her hand. "I'm sorry. It's not your fault you work for a dictator. Yes, please. Coffee would be lovely."

Coffee turned out to be breakfast. Juice, toast, fruit, eggs, bacon. Sam ignored everything but the toast and the coffee. Cosimia had brought two cups. Did that mean the Great Man himself was going to put in an appearance? Was she supposed to wait for his permission to leave this room?

The hell with that.

Sam lifted the tray from her lap, put it on the nightstand and took a long look around her. Bed, nightstand, chair, dresser. She could make it from one piece of furniture to the other, then to the door, and figure out the rest when she had to deal with it.

She flung back the blanket, stood up and balanced carefully on her good leg. Yes. It would work. She was not helpless. Did Demetrios think she would be? Was he still ticked off because she'd walked out instead of taking his orders? And had he forgotten he'd arranged a meeting for this morning? She remembered that, clearly enough. She remembered everything that had gone on in those last humiliating minutes in the conference room, how he'd barked at her, how he'd—

"What in hell do you think you're doing?"

Sam let out a thin shriek, swung towards the door, overbalanced, windmilled her arms and toppled backwards. Demetrios cursed, sprang towards her and caught her just before she went down.

"You are an impossible woman," he said furiously. "And you cannot be trusted."

"I'm impossible?" Sam shot back. "That's great, coming from you. I wake up in a strange bed, in a strange room, my ankle trussed up like a—a lamb chop ready for the skillet, with no clothes, no cane, no way to so much as get from the bed to the bathroom on my own, and *I'm* impossible?" She glared at him. "Please put me down."

"With pleasure."

He dropped her onto the bed, put his hands on his hips and eyed her coldly. So much for the sweet, soft woman who'd sighed in his arms last night.

"I regret the accommodations aren't to your liking, Miss Brewster. It was the best I could do on short notice. Next time, perhaps, you might consider announcing that you intend to sprain your ankle in advance."

"Oh, that's really funny." Sam huffed out a breath,

folded her arms and considered the situation. "I suppose," she said grudgingly, "I should thank you."

"For what? The fact that you feel like a lamb chop? Please, don't bother."

"Look, maybe I went overboard just now. The thing is, I—I was feeling a little sorry for myself. And then you came into the room and scared the dickens out of me." She sighed, looked up. "And—and—"

"And?" Demetrios demanded, but Sam's brain had stopped functioning.

She'd never seen him like this, casually dressed in faded jeans and a snug, equally faded black T-shirt. His feet were shoved into a pair of moccasins that looked as if they'd been around for quite a while. His dark hair was damp, his jaw was shadowed with stubble, and not even the glower on his face could change the fact that he was early morning gorgeous.

Or that memories were returning. Demetrios, his hands on her skin. His breath mingling with hers. His arms holding her close...

"And?" he said again.

"And," she said slowly, "I apologize. I shouldn't have snapped your head off."

Nothing changed in the way he was looking at her, not for what seemed forever. Then, gradually, a smile began at the corners of his mouth.

"Apology accepted." He nodded at the tray on the nightstand. "I thought we could have our coffee together."

"Don't you have a meeting this morning?"

"I canceled it. How do you feel?"

"Better. Well, my ankle's not good enough to walk on, but—"

"No walking. The doctor says you're to stay off that ankle for a couple of days. It needs time to heal."

"The thing is..." She hesitated. "The thing is... I don't seem to be able to remember much about last night."

Was she imagining things or did two bands of pink suddenly stripe his cheeks? "There isn't much to remember," he said briskly. "Is that coffee still hot?"

"I'm sure it is. But—"

He sat down beside her on the bed, his thigh just brushing hers. There were layers between them, her robe and his jeans; there was the silk duvet and its matching top sheet, but she could feel the point of their contact burn like a hot iron. Carefully, she drew her leg away from his.

He poured his coffee, topped off hers, and smiled at her. "Cosimia has made you comfortable?"

"Is this your room?"

"You have a habit of answering a question with a question."

"Is it?"

He nodded. "Yes."

"Why?"

"Why, what? Why are you here and not in the cottage?" He shrugged, drank some of his coffee. "It seemed unwise to leave you alone in case your ankle troubled you during the night. That turned out to be a good idea, because you had a strong reaction to the medication the doctor gave you."

"Reaction?" Now her loss of memory was beginning to make sense. "Was it codeine?"

He nodded, gave her a little smile. "It made you drunk."

"Floaty."

"Yes. That was what you said. I phoned the doctor when I realized what was happening. He said you'd be fine as soon as you slept it off."

"I remember now. The nurse gave me some pills… I only took codeine once, when I was a little girl. I took a tumble—"

"—and broke your leg after Billy Riley dared you to use a rope swing over the river." Demetrios smiled. "I know."

"You know?" Sam stared at him. "I told you about that?"

He shrugged. "As you say, you were—"

"Floaty," she said quickly. "Exactly. I don't remember anything after you took me to the hospital."

"There isn't much to remember."

His voice was a little rough and she could sense a tension in him. Something had happened; something had changed. If only she could remember...

"I brought you home. To my house."

"Your house." Her voice shook and she cleared her throat. "And—and to your room?"

"My room. And my bed." He put his cup on the tray, then took hers and put it there, too. "Samantha. I want you to remember last night. I want you to remember all of it."

"Demetrios—"

"Do you know how long I've waited to hear you say my name?" He moved closer to her, framed her face with his hands. "I see more questions in your eyes, *gataki*. Ask them. You want to know why I put you here and not in one of the other bedrooms. You want to know who put you to bed and who took care of you." A muscle knotted in his jaw. "Ask, and I will give you the answers—or are you afraid to hear them? Would you prefer we went on with this silly pretense?"

"What pretense? I don't know what you're talking about."

He nodded. He'd expected that she would choose not to know what had happened. What she felt. What she wanted. Why would he want her to? It was foolish to pursue a woman who preferred a lie to the truth when there were so many others who were eager to acknowledge desire. The world was filled with women who could be easily seduced.

Except, he didn't want any of them. He wanted this one, who was afraid to admit her need for him. He didn't fully understand her fear but he was willing to confront it because, in the grayness of early morning, he'd admitted a truth of his own.

He was afraid, too.

After he'd left her, he'd gone to his library, watched the

sun feather the sky with pink and fuchsia while he drank bad coffee he'd made himself because not even the cook had been awake at that hour. Alone, he'd contemplated the sunrise as if he'd never seen it before. It had been in the way of a lesson, reminding him that the sun would rise tomorrow and all the tomorrows after that, even if neither he or she acknowledged what had happened in that bedroom.

Every instinct had warned him to do the sensible thing, greet Samantha politely when she awakened and pretend the way she'd sighed in his arms was nothing but a dream. They'd struck sparks against each other from the beginning but he'd lived long enough to know that sparks could as easily sputter and die as they could blaze into a conflagration.

Yes, he'd decided, forgetting what had gone on in that bedroom was the best solution.

He'd poured himself another cup of coffee—drinkable, this time, because the cook had made it. He'd climbed the stairs, prepared to smile and say the right thing…and saw Samantha, sitting up in his bed, wearing his robe, and he'd wondered how he could have imagined letting her leave him until they'd faced what they felt and saw it through to its inevitable end. Even as he'd thought it, she'd tossed back the covers, lurched to her feet, that damnable independence of hers driving her to risk her injured ankle…

"I never would have imagined you to be a coward," he said huskily.

"You're wasting your time." Her voice was strong but she hadn't tried to move away. She was trembling under his hands. "Do you really think you can trick me into another silly challenge? Frankly, I don't give a damn whether I woke up in your bed or—"

"I brought you into my house because you needed someone to watch over you. Cosimia suggested I put you in one of the guest suites. She offered to sleep in the room with you." Demetrios took a deep breath. "I said no. Do you know why?"

"Yes," she said fiercely. "You said 'no' because you can't imagine not being in charge of everything and everyone. You have to control the world, Demetrios, and I don't like men who—"

He covered her mouth with his, silencing her with his kiss.

"Please," she whispered, even as she raised her hands and curled them into his shirt, "I beg you. Don't do this. Don't say any more."

"I wanted to be with you, to be the one you turned to in the night." He lifted her face and forced her to meet his eyes. "I undressed you, *gataki*. I put you to bed. And I held you in my arms most of the night, after you begged me not to leave you."

Sam drew an unsteady breath. She'd known it. Sensed it. Recalled it all happening, if not as a memory than as something burned into her very soul.

"No more lies, *matyá mou*, not for either of us." He slid his hands down her back, then gathered her to him. "We made a bad bargain that day in New York. We thought the challenge of working together would be enough to quench the fire of what we felt but it isn't. I want you more than ever, now that I know you. And you want me."

"We agreed—"

"Yes. We did." He lowered his forehead to hers. "If you tell me, I will walk out of this room and never mention any of this again."

She said nothing. He waited, hearing the beat of his own heart, seeing the blurring in her eyes. He could make her admit the truth; he knew that as surely as he'd seen the sun rise this morning. All it would take would be a caress. A kiss. He could breach all her defenses with a touch but he wanted more than that. He needed her to come to him. To reach for him.

She made a little sound, closed her eyes, caught her lip

between her teeth. He could feel his resolve slipping. To hold her in his arms, to feel her warmth and not make love to her, was rapidly becoming impossible. He reminded himself, once again, that he was a man and not a saint…but if he spent many more moments like this, he might yet become one.

Enough, he thought, and let go of her.

"I release you from our contract," he said softly. "I will pay you the full amount we agreed upon, *gataki*. You may leave for the States as soon as your ankle is healed."

"Demetrios—"

"No. It's all right." He rose from the bed and walked to the door, a man destined for sainthood and already damning himself for it.

"Please. Don't go."

Her voice was soft but it stopped his heart. He turned and looked at her, saw her lips curve in a smile so intimate, so filled with promise, it almost brought him to his knees. Slowly, so slowly that it seemed to take forever, she opened the robe. The edges parted; he saw the rounded curves of her breasts and the gentle rise of her belly.

"Come to me," she whispered.

Sam held out her arms. Demetrios turned the lock and went to claim the woman who had surely been his from the very beginning of time.

CHAPTER EIGHT

HE WAS beautiful.

Sam had never imagined using that word to describe a man but as Demetrios stripped off his shirt, she knew it was the only word that suited him.

His shoulders were wide, his arms powerfully muscled. An inverted vee of dark, silky hair stretched over his chest and arrowed down to his navel. Clothed, he'd looked like a man of civility and power but she'd always sensed the darker, more primitive side of him.

Now, as he came towards her, bare-chested, the top button of his jeans undone, his eyes dark and fixed on hers, she knew that this was the real Demetrios Karas. He was a man who took what he wanted—and what he wanted was her.

The realization was more exciting than anything she'd ever known. She could feel her body readying itself for his. Her nipples were tight with desire, her breasts almost aching with it. A heaviness seemed to settle low in her belly.

"Demetrios," she whispered, as he reached her.

"Yes, sweetheart," he said softly. "I know. We've waited a long time for this."

She trembled as he slid the robe from her shoulders, moaned when he dipped his head and pressed his lips to her throat. Could he feel the hammer of her pulse against his mouth? He was whispering to her in Greek. She didn't understand all the words. She didn't have to. The brush of his hands, the way he clasped her shoulders, was an eloquent language all its own.

His hands cupped her face. When he took her mouth with his, she could taste the dark, smoky passion he held in such tight control. He was being gentle for her but that wasn't what she wanted. Not from him. She wanted everything he was, everything he could make her feel, and she wound her arms around his neck as she opened her mouth to his and moved against him. He groaned, caught her wrists and brought her hands against his chest. She could feel the tremor of his muscles beneath her fingertips.

"Sam. I don't want to hurt you, *gataki.* Your ankle—"

She answered by tugging a hand free, skimming it down his jeans and closing her fingers over his erection, reveling in the life and heat that pulsed at her touch.

"I want this," she whispered. "I want you, deep inside me."

He could feel his composure slipping away; he was closer to losing himself than he had been since he was a boy. Quickly, he shucked off his jeans. Sam had a fleeting glimpse of all that magnificent male power, and then she was in his arms again, with his mouth on her breast, suckling her, nipping her, tonguing her until suddenly she gave a high, keening cry and she came, came just from this.

Demetrios held her to him as she arched against him, her cries almost feral in their intensity, and even though he was shaking he told himself not to let go. Not yet. He wanted more, to know that she was lost to the world, to rational thought, to everything but him. Only him, and he swept his hand down her body, cupped the strip of silk between her thighs.

"No more," she moaned, "I can't…"

But she could. He took her higher and higher, pressing one finger into the silk, into the soft cleft of her womanhood, seeking and finding the sweet, engorged bud that awaited him. He tore the silk away, touched her, stroked her, bent to her and took her mouth so that her cries became part of him.

The pulse of her climax rocketed through him. He was damp with sweat; his muscles trembling. Still he held back, watching her, exulting in what he had done to her, for her, and then he entered her, moved, moved again. This time, when she sobbed his name, Demetrios let go and followed Sam into a spiraling explosion of light.

Sam didn't move. She never wanted to move again.

She'd never experienced anything like what had just happened. All that passion. All that heat. And now, this. Lying beneath Demetrios, his mouth at her throat, his arms hard around her, his body pressing against hers…

Her blood still hummed with pleasure. She sighed, ran her hands down his back, luxuriating in the firmness of his muscles, the dampness of his skin. Long moments slipped past. Then he lifted his head, kissed her temple and began to move away.

She tightened her arms around him. "No. Don't go."

"I'm too heavy for you," he said softly.

"I like the feel of you against me." She kissed his throat. "Stay here. Please."

She had said almost the same thing to him last night and he would no more have left her then than he would now. Holding her, he rolled to his side, cradling her against him so they still touched, breast to breast, belly to belly. Gently, he slid his hand under her knee, lifted her leg and brought it across his hip.

"Does your ankle hurt?"

"What ankle?" Sam laughed softly. "You're much better for aches and pains than codeine."

Demetrios smiled, threaded his fingers into her hair and kissed the tip of her nose. "I'm sure the medical journals would be pleased to learn that, *gataki*. Seriously, are you all right? I promised the doctor I'd take good care of you."

"And you have." She smiled as she stroked his dark hair from his forehead. "You've kept me off my foot, haven't you?"

"Mmm." He bent his head to her breast, licked the nipple until it pebbled. "I told him it would take great effort, that you would need to be kept occupied."

Sam gave a soft moan as he slipped his hand between her thighs. "Great effort," she whispered.

Demetrios lifted his head and looked at her face. Her skin was flushed, her lips parted with desire as he caressed her. He felt his hardened flesh stir, his arousal heighten with the need to make love to her again.

"Shall I think of a way to keep you busy?" he said softly.

"I think…" Her lips parted for his kiss. "I think that's a fine—"

He kissed her slowly, deeply, and moved over her again. She saw the intensity in his eyes, the way the bones in his face stood out in stark relief, and something hot and dangerous skittered in her blood, something that was more than desire, more than she was ready for.

He kissed her again, kissed her breasts, her belly. She wanted to tell him to stop. She wanted to tell him never to stop, to go on making love to her until neither of them could move.

"Demetrios," she whispered, her voice breaking, and what he heard in the way she sighed his name shook him to the depths of his soul.

"Samantha. *O kalóz mou,*" he said, as he put his hands under her, lifted her to his mouth, tasted the honeyed sweetness that was for him. Only for him. She came, hard and fast, and he moved up her body as she did, slid deep inside her and took her up and up again until she was weeping with the beauty of what she felt, with the knowledge that this was all she'd ever wanted, this man, this one man, forever…

Sam stopped thinking and gave herself up to Demetrios's possession.

She awoke alone in his bed.

Hours had passed; late afternoon sunlight streamed into the room, filling it with a hot golden glow.

Sam stretched, yawned, caught her breath as she inadvertently flexed her ankle. The rest of her felt wonderful.

She smiled and flung her arms over her head. She'd imagined how it would be, to make love with Demetrios, but nothing she'd imagined came anywhere near the truth. He was an incredible lover. Wild. Tender. Demanding. Generous. Just remembering made her body grow warm and soft with need.

Sam rolled onto her belly.

But she'd complicated things. She knew that. Yesterday, he'd been her employer. Now, he was her lover. The delicate balance between man and woman had changed. What would happen now? What would he expect?

She'd always been careful to keep the personal part of her life separate from the professional. Men had a way of thinking that sexual intimacy gave them the right to take over your existence. It was only logical that sleeping with the man you worked with would make things even more difficult.

Of course, some women seemed to enjoy having a protective male hovering over them. If that was their thing, fine. Sam couldn't understand it, but who was she to sit in judgment? But to fall in love with a man like that...

Fall in love? Where had that come from?

Frowning, she sat up and pushed her hair back from her face. What had happened in this bed had nothing to do with love. Love was an illusion. A pleasant one, for as long as it lasted, but as far as she could see it was just a way of pretending you hadn't offered your independence up like a gift.

There wasn't much difference between a man's involvement in a woman's life and his eventual domination of it. She'd come close to telling that to Carin once. Her sister had been cheerfully explaining that she'd like to come to New York for a visit but first she'd have to check with Rafe.

"You need his permission?" Sam had said and even though she'd tried to mask her distaste, she knew she hadn't succeeded because Carin had laughed and said no, of course she didn't.

"But I wouldn't just take off without discussing it with him, Sam. Surely, you can understand that."

"What I understand," Sam had replied, "is that there was a time you thought for yourself."

"I'm going to let that pass because I love you," Carin had said, still laughing but with an edge to her tone. "Rafe would do the same thing for me. We have a responsibility to each other. We don't live separate lives. Nobody does, once they're married. Not if the marriage is going to work."

Not if you didn't mind signing your life over to a man, was what she'd meant, but Sam had decided to keep quiet. What her sisters called responsibility, she called dependency but, hey, if Carin and Amanda wanted to delude themselves into calling it love, who was she to spoil things for them?

And what on earth was she doing, plunging into such deep philosophical water this morning? She'd made love with Demetrios. She hadn't fallen in love with him. It was just that she'd never gone to bed with a man like him before. There was something about the way he'd taken charge that was different. There was no harm in admitting that to herself. They'd been equals in this bed but a little part of her had always been aware of the differences, of his strength and her softness, his masculinity and her femininity. He'd been gentle one moment, fierce the next. And he'd made her feel something—something she'd never sensed in herself before, something that lurked just at the edge of logic and made her heartbeat quicken, even now.

Whoa. First philosophy, then introspection. Enough, she thought, and tossed back the covers. Demetrios's robe lay at the foot of the bed. She grabbed it and put it on.

What she'd just experienced was the best sex of her life. Why try and put a gloss to something so basic? She wasn't a woman who'd ever shied away from the truth; she'd never been silly enough to think sex was only a matter of connecting Body Part A and Body Part B. Emotion was everything. You had to like a man, respect him, to sleep with him, but you certainly didn't have to dream of forever after.

"Sam?"

The sound of Demetrios's voice startled her. She turned and saw him standing in the doorway. He was wearing his jeans but his chest was bare; the stubble on his jaw had darkened. He was glowering at her and she knew it was because she was sitting up, with both her feet on the floor, that she'd ignored what he thought was advice and she considered orders...and she couldn't work up the anger she knew his attitude deserved.

All she could think of was that she wanted him again, with a need that was frightening.

What had she gotten herself into?

He was all wrong for her. If a fairy godmother had suddenly dropped from the sky and said, "Here you go, Sam, take this pen and paper and make up a list of the things you want in a man," nothing on that list would remotely describe him. He was too good-looking. Good-looking men were conceited and if he didn't seem to be, now that she'd gotten to know him, surely it was only a matter of time before she discovered that he was.

Besides, he was too everything else. Macho. Demanding. Possessive. He was a man who'd drive her crazy, wanting to protect her from everything...

And she was as wrong for him as he was for her.

Was that why they'd wanted each other so badly? She'd never been with a man like him, and she'd have bet every dollar she owned that she was the exact opposite of any of the women he knew. She wasn't docile. She had her own life. She made her own decisions, and she'd never, ever be content to live in a man's shadow—except, that was already happening.

One night in Demetrios's bed, one morning as his lover, and he was in charge. She was damned near a prisoner in his room. No clothes. No cane. No choice but to be completely dependent on him, and now he was closing the door, standing there with his arms folded and a look on his face as if she'd committed the crime of the century, all because she'd decided not to wait for him to tell her it was okay to swing her feet to the floor.

"Surely, you know better than to try and put weight on that foot," he said.

"Surely, you know better than to tell me what to do."

His eyebrows rose. He looked at her as if she'd lost her mind but if she had, she'd recovered it.

"And you might have knocked before coming into the room. I know this is your bedroom, but—"

"What has this to do with bedrooms? You cannot put weight on that leg."

"I'm not an idiot, Demetrios. I'll be careful."

"You *are* an idiot, if you think I'm going to permit you to stand up."

"Permit me?" Sam lurched to her feet. Her ankle popped. The sound was so loud and hideous that she felt her stomach rise into her throat but she forced herself not to so much as flinch. "I don't require your permission. Not for anything."

"Sam." He smiled as he came towards her. She could almost see the gears turning inside that handsome, all-too-sure-of-itself head. If scolding a kitten didn't work, you tried kindness. "I understand, sweetheart."

"You couldn't possibly."

"But I do. Your ankle hurts. You feel irritable. You need a change of scene."

"Yes, and I'm going to have one." She took a breath, gritted her teeth, reached for the back of a chair and hobbled towards it. "Thank you for everything, but—"

"Get back in the bed, Samantha."

The smile was gone. His face might have been carved from marble. So much for kindness.

"No."

"I leave you for five minutes, and what happens?"

"I took my life back," she said brusquely, "that's what happens."

"And what is that supposed to mean?"

"Look, I'm very grateful for all your help, but—"

"Grateful?"

"Yes. You've been very kind, Demetrios, but—"

"First, you thank me. Now you tell me that I have been very kind." His voice was low and filled with warning. "Perhaps you would like to shake my hand."

"I'm only trying to tell you that—that I'm—"

"Grateful. So you said." His eyes narrowed until she could see only a flash of stormy blue. "Is that why you slept with me? Out of gratitude?"

"You get the hell out of here!"

"It's a reasonable assumption. Perhaps it's simpler to roll around under a man than to write a thank-you note."

She sprang at him, her fist balled and drawn back, but he caught her in his arms before she could take a swing.

"Damn you!" Struggling against him was useless but she struggled anyway, until she was panting with frustration. "Put me down!"

"Where? In your cottage, away from me? Or perhaps you'd prefer I send for a taxi to take you to the airport so you can fly back to the States. Would putting five thousand miles between us make you feel safe?"

"Safe? Safe? What's that supposed to mean?"

"You know precisely what it means," he growled. "You are afraid."

"I've never been afraid of anything in my life!"

Demetrios looked down into Sam's flushed face. Dammit, how could she turn him into a crazy man with just a couple of words? He was always good with women, calm even in the face of their admittedly mercurial temperaments, but he couldn't seem to keep his anger leashed with this one.

"You're afraid of me," he said.

"Afraid? Of you? Trust me, mister, you flatter yourself if you imagine I'm the least bit intimidated by your temper or your money or your size. And if you don't let go of me—"

He muttered a word in Greek, bent his head and took her mouth with his. When she gasped and tried to twist away, he sank his hand into her hair and kept her where he wanted her until he was good and ready to end the kiss. This was what she needed. A man she couldn't order around. A man who could dominate her, control her...

Want her with each breath, each beat of his heart.

"That's what you're afraid of," he said roughly. "Me, and what I make you feel."

Sam glared at him. "You're insane."

"If I am, it's your doing."

"You see? You really are—you really are—"

He kissed her again, this time gently, his mouth moving softly against hers. When he drew back, there were tears in her eyes.

"I hate you," she said unsteadily. "I really, really hate—"

He kissed her again and she moaned, put her arms around him and kissed him back. By the time they tumbled to the bed together, her legs were around his hips and he was sheathed deep inside her.

The world, and everything in it, no longer existed.

There was only this room, and each other.

Demetrios stirred, groaned, opened his eyes, then shut them again.

"I think I'm dying," he said.

Sam laughed softly. She lay in the curve of his arm, her body sprawled over his. "Can you guess what *I'm* thinking?"

"I'm afraid to ask," he said, but she could hear the smile in his voice.

"Not that." She folded her hands on the swell of his chest and propped her chin on her knuckles. "You haven't shaved."

"I will, as soon as I recover. Say, in five or ten years."

"That wasn't a complaint. I like the feel of your beard."

"It's stubble."

"What's the difference?"

"My father had a beard. I have stubble."

She traced the hard line of his jaw with one finger. It drifted close to his mouth and he caught it between his teeth and sucked gently. "And if you keep doing that, my recovery may take less time than I thought."

"Don't you want to know what I'm thinking?"

He could feel her body growing softer, more pliant. His was hardening. How was that possible? He'd lost count of how many times they'd made love.

"I already know," he said, and moved his hips.

She kissed his chest. He could feel her mouth curve in a smile.

"What I'm thinking about is...let's see. First, a shower."

"Mmm." Demetrios gathered her closer in his arms, stroked one hand the length of her spine. "That can be arranged."

"And then—" She sighed. His touch made her want to curl up against him. It also made her want to ravish him. Could you do both at once? It was an interesting postulate. "And then," she murmured, "I want something to eat."

"Uh-huh." He trailed a hand over her bottom, loving the sweet curves that were warm beneath his palm. "Would that involve whipped cream?"

Sam laughed. "It involves a big steak. Or a dozen scrambled eggs. Or even a peanut butter sandwich."

"Peanut butter." He shuddered. "I knew I'd finally learn something terrible about you." He slid his hands up to her shoulders, raised her towards him and kissed her. "Are you telling me you need sustenance, madam?"

"Such a clever man."

He kissed her again, more deeply. "At this very moment? Or could you wait for just a little while?"

She sat up, her knees on either side of his hips, her smile filled with temptation. "I'm not sure," she said softly. "Would you like to explain my options?"

God, how he loved to look at her. Especially when they made love. When he cupped her breasts, as he was doing now. Stroked her aroused flesh. He loved the way her eyes turned black. The way her breathing quickened. The way her skin took on a glaze, like the petals of a cream-colored rose under the kiss of early morning dew.

She was beautiful, this woman rising above him like a goddess.

He rolled his thumbs across her nipples. She sighed his name and he ran his hand over her belly, tried to decide which he wanted more, to enter her again or just to pull her down into his arms and kiss her sweet, swollen mouth.

What was happening to him?

He was hardly a sexual novice. There'd been women in his life since Christmas vacation in his fifteenth year when his father had given him a Lamborghini he was too young to drive and the upstairs maid had given him herself, which he wasn't. He knew all about sex and took modest pride in knowing he'd never failed to please a woman, but to want one with such ceaseless yearning? To make love to her over and over, and then to find himself erect and wanting her again, when his brain told him such a thing was anatomically impossible?

Why question such a miracle?

And yet he'd questioned it this morning. He'd awakened with Sam in his arms and his mind, and the joy he'd felt had scared the hell out of him.

He'd never wanted a woman to the exclusion of everything else. He'd canceled today's meeting, made, instead, tentative plans for lunch...and forgotten all about them, now that he thought about it. That was what he'd come upstairs to tell Sam, that the morning had been wonderful and he wanted her to stay here and rest while he went into Piraeus, to meet with his colleagues...and then he'd stepped into the room, found her on her feet and ready to do battle, and he'd been torn between wanting to shake her until her teeth rattled and kissing her until she understood—

Understood what? Hell, *he* didn't understand. How could she?

He only knew that ships and shipyards didn't matter, when he could have this. This, he thought, groaning as she put her hand on him, stroked him from the tip to the base of his straining erection. And this, he thought, as he clasped her hips, lifted her, then slowly brought her down onto his rigid flesh. Her head fell back; her shudder seemed to go straight through his bloodstream, into his heart.

"Sam," he said, "Sam…"

The words were so close, so near, but he let them spin away. Let the world spin away, in a torrent of sensation.

He was almost unbearably gentle when he unwound the elastic bandage.

"Does this hurt?" he kept asking, "Does that?"

"No," Sam told him, but he didn't believe her and finally she threatened to hobble into the shower on her own.

He swung her into his arms, carried her into the bathroom, fussed over giving her a few minutes of privacy.

"Call me if you feel weak," he said, and Sam rolled her eyes and said the only thing that would make her feel weak would be the sight of a peanut butter sandwich instead of a rare steak and a huge baked potato within the next half hour.

When she was done, Demetrios carried her into the shower though she insisted she was perfectly capable of getting there on her own.

"No," he replied, in a tone that would have set her hackles on end just a little while ago.

He bathed her and that took time, lots of time, because there were so many sweet, hidden places that needed his very personal attention. Eventually, he wrapped a towel around his waist, wrapped one around her, and carried her to the bedroom where she was surprised to see some of her own clothes—underwear, shorts, T-shirt—lying on the neatly made bed.

"I phoned down to Cosimia, while you were in the bathroom," he said with a studied nonchalance that made Sam's nerve endings go on alert.

"Oh." She sank down on the edge of the bed, clutching at the towel. It was ridiculous to feel modest but she did. Cosimia knew they were lovers? She would, of course; they'd been in this room for hours. Still, she wasn't accustomed to sharing bits of her private life with others. "It was kind of her to bring me something to wear."

Demetrios nodded. He seemed nervous. Sam wondered why.

"It is warm out," he said.

Yes, definitely nervous. There was that accent of his again. It came and went like the tide.

"So the shorts should be fine, but it you prefer something else…"

"No, no. This is perfect. There's no reason for Cosimia to go all the way back to the guest cottage."

"She would not have to." He took a breath. "All of your things are here."

Sam stared at him blankly. "What do you mean?"

"I mean that I told her to pack everything." He waved towards the wall of closets. "Your clothing is there, kitten. So if you wish to choose something else to wear—"

"But why? I live in—"

"This is where you will live, from now on. In this house. This room. With me."

His tone had become tight and cool. She knew he expected a fight and that she was damned well going to oblige him.

"Did it ever occur to you to ask me if that was what I wanted?"

"No." Demetrios folded his arms and looked down at her, his expression shuttered. "It did not."

She wanted to hit him. She'd never hit anybody in her life—well, not unless you counted the Riley kid—and now, twice within who knew how long, she'd wanted to slug Demetrios Karas. This was exactly what she'd been afraid of, that he'd make all kinds of assumptions just because they'd slept together.

"Well, it should have because I'd have said, no, I do not want to share your room. I do not want you making decisions for me. I do not want—"

"What you *want*," he said, squatting down before her and clasping her shoulders, "is me. And I want you. Why is that so difficult to admit?"

"Do not, for even a moment, assume you can think for me!" Sam pushed against his chest. "I have never once lived with a man, and I'm not about to start now."

"Nor have I lived with a woman."

"I'll bet. You really want me to believe you've never had a woman unpack her things and settle in here?"

"Absolutely. No woman has awakened in this bed until today."

"You've never had a mistress?"

He took a deep breath. "Yes, I have had mistresses." He felt her tense under his hands and he held her harder, determined to make her listen. "But they have not lived with me. I have not awakened in the morning and shared breakfast with them in this house. I have not gone to sleep at night in my own bed, knowing that the woman who will be in my arms the next morning will have a shiny face free of makeup. I have never wanted that."

"And now you do?" Sam's voice shook and she hated herself for it, for wanting to believe him and wanting to throw herself into his arms when she knew, she *knew*, that it was a terrible mistake.

"Yes, *o kalóz mou*, I do."

His arms went around her but she held herself rigid. She could almost see her life shifting, the path that had once run straight and smooth already taking a twisting turn.

"What does that mean? What you just called me? *Kalóz mou.*"

"It means 'beloved,'" he said softly, and kissed her, and what could she do after that but put her arms around his neck and kiss him back?

CHAPTER NINE

IT WAS a long, lazy weekend, spent in and out of bed.

Demetrios plied her with cool drinks and concern. Was the elastic bandage too loose? Too tight? Did she want an ice pack? Aspirin?

Sam assured him she was fine. And when, in early evening, they began to dress for dinner and, instead, made love yet again, he stopped and said he should have thought of asking, but he'd assumed...was she protected? She said yes, she was, and drew him back into her arms.

She'd always preferred being responsible for herself in all possible ways. That was why she took birth control pills, even when she wasn't involved with anybody. She'd forgotten to take one last night but that wasn't a problem. Taking a double dose, once she'd realized it, made up for the lapse.

Late Saturday evening, they took the helicopter into Athens and drove to a small café for dinner.

"You will like this place," Demetrios said, as they sped along a winding road high above the sea.

"I will like this place," Sam echoed, and rolled her eyes. "It's nice to see that little touch of uncertainty."

He flashed her a quick grin. "You'll see, *kalóz mou.* I'm right."

He was. The café was small, the view incredible, the food wonderful. And their entrance stopped conversation.

"I'll bet it isn't every night a man carries his dinner date through the door," Sam said, after they were seated.

Demetrios laughed. "We may have started a new trend."

"Well, we're going to end that trend. I want a cane."

"You prefer a cane to the very personalized service

127

you're getting from me?'' He slapped his hand to his heart. ''I'm devastated.''

''No,'' Sam said, smiling across the small table, ''you're not. I'm serious, Demetrios. I want a cane. I need to be able to get around on my own.''

It turned out the gardener still had a cane he'd used a few years ago. Demetrios claimed he hadn't thought of mentioning it and besides, it would be useless on stairs because it no longer had a rubber tip, which was why she had to let him carry her through the house and out to the pool on Sunday morning.

She clung to his neck and tried to work up some anger or at least some irritation but the truth was that it was nice to feel so cherished. Still, she protested when he put her down gently on a chaise longue and told her she could get some sun while he did his laps.

''Do you really expect me to lie here like a potato, baking in the sun?''

''I like your swimsuit,'' he said. ''What there is of it.''

''You're changing the subject.''

''A woman who wears three small triangles and calls it a swimsuit runs that risk.''

Sam sighed. ''It's a bikini.''

''It's a risk to a man's health.''

She gave up. How could she quarrel with a man who was looking at her as he was? She smiled and looped her arms around his neck.

''I'm glad you like it. I tossed it into my luggage at the last minute.''

''Ah. So you planned on basking on the beach, even as you accepted my job offer?''

''Of course.''

''Did you think of me when you packed it?''

He grinned. Sam grinned back.

''I thought of Saint Tropez. That's where I bought it.''

He touched a finger lightly to one slender strap. ''Most of the good beaches in Saint Tropez are nude.''

"I know. I couldn't bring myself to go nude, so I bought this instead."

Demetrios slid a finger under the strap and drew it down her shoulder. "And? Did it help?"

"Oh, definitely." She laughed. "But not in the way I expected. I felt totally self-conscious. I was the only woman wearing a suit. So, after a few minutes, I took it off."

"You took it off," he said solemnly, and told himself it was ridiculous to feel jealous of any man who had seen her that day. "How?"

"What do you mean, how? I just—Demetrios?" She caught his hand as he undid the clasp and slipped the top of the bikini from her shoulders.

"Yes?"

His voice had roughened. She could see a muscle ticking in his cheek, see the darkness in his eyes, a darkness she had learned could sweep her away.

"Someone might see us," she whispered as he cupped her breasts in his hands.

"No one will see us." He bent his head and she moaned as he put his mouth to her flesh. "The cypresses that ring the pool are thick, *kalóz mou*. We are as alone here as we would be in bed."

She lay back, lifted her hips as he freed her of the thong bottom, watched through narrowed eyes as he skimmed off his trunks. He had done it again, ignored what she said, but as he gathered her to him all that mattered was the feel of him in her arms while the warm Aegean breeze sighed through the trees.

Monday morning, Sam opened her eyes and saw the cane leaning against the nightstand, complete with rubber tip.

She saw Demetrios, too. He was standing before the mirror, fully dressed, adjusting his tie.

She sat up, holding the covers to her breasts. "Did I oversleep?"

He turned around. She felt a chill whip through her blood.

He was smiling, but there was something removed in the way he looked at her.

"No. Not at all. I just thought it would be easier if I showered and dressed first."

"Yes. Of course." She looked at the cane. "I see you found the tip for the cane."

He shrugged. "The gardener found it."

"Ah. Well—well, I'll have to thank him."

"I already did. We couldn't very well start the morning's meeting with me carrying you into the conference room, could we?" He smiled again, then turned back to the mirror. "I'm going to get some coffee. Phone down when you're ready and I'll come help you down the stairs." His eyes met hers in the mirror. He looked at her for a long moment, his expression impossible to read. "That is, if I'm right and you intend to go to work today...?"

"Certainly." Sam felt her throat constrict. Still holding the covers, she swung her feet to the floor. "Why would you even ask?"

"Why, indeed?" He smiled, made one last adjustment to his tie and left the room.

The door swung shut. Sam stared after it, then took a deep breath. Was it all over? Just one weekend, and he'd had enough of her? She leaned on the nightstand, reached for the cane and hobbled to the bathroom. It didn't seem possible, not after last night. They'd made love for hours.

But just before they fell asleep, she'd remembered that the next day was Monday. And she'd known, with a little start of surprise, that she didn't want to go to the office. She wanted to be alone with Demetrios. She'd started to tell him that...and then she'd thought, what if he didn't feel the same way? So she'd said, lightly, "Don't forget to set the alarm clock," and held her breath, waiting for him to say he didn't give a damn about the clock, or work, or anything except her.

But hadn't. He'd reached for the clock, shot her a quick smile and said he was just going to do that.

It was foolish, that such a thing should have bothered her. They were business colleagues first, lovers second. They weren't even supposed to be lovers... And yet, she hadn't wanted him to set the damned clock. And she certainly hadn't wanted to wake up and find him dressed. She'd wanted to awaken in his arms, to hear him say he didn't give a damn about time or work or anything but her...

What kind of idiocy was that? She had a job to do and she would do it. And if Demetrios had changed his mind about wanting her in his life, he was going to have to look her in the eye and say so. She'd be perfectly content to go back to the guest house and to her normal life.

If the great Demetrios Karas thought she was going to plead with him to want her, he was wrong.

Demetrios stood in the kitchen, sipping his coffee.

If Samantha thought he was going to plead with her to ask him to cancel today's meeting, she was wrong.

He'd thought of doing it the instant he woke, then dismissed the idea as nonsense. He'd never done such a thing in his life. These were important meetings, and he had always born his responsibilities well. He was the son of a father who'd started as a deckhand on a tramp steamer and ended up owning that ship and a fleet of others, a man who knew that hard work and risk came first.

It was an admirable heritage, one to live up to, and Demetrios always had.

Still, one more canceled meeting more would not ruin anything.

He'd looked at Sam's face, only a breath from his. Would she think that it would be far more important to spend another day alone than to sit in a room filled with other people and pretend to keep her mind on business? She was so serious about her work. Not that he didn't admire her. It was an admirable quality in a woman—but other things suddenly seemed to matter more.

He'd gazed at her for a long time, watching her as she

slept curled on her side next to him. How beautiful she was. Such long lashes. Such a sweet mouth. Carefully, he drew down the covers, saw the gentle fullness of her breast, the curve of her hip...

And ached to touch her. Just one touch. One kiss, and he knew what would happen, that she would awaken, smile, go into his arms...

And tell him today was a business day.

Why had he even imagined she'd want to forget the world and stay here, with him? Last night, after they'd made love and he was about to turn out the light, she'd asked him if he'd set the alarm clock. The question had caught him by surprise, and he hadn't been sure how it made him feel. Part of him had loved the way she'd said it, as if they'd been sleeping together forever. Part of him tensed at the realization that she'd think of business after the weekend they'd spent.

"I was just going to do that," he'd said, even though it wasn't true. All he'd been thinking of was taking her in his arms and going to sleep, holding her close.

He'd remembered all that early this morning and he'd lost the desire to kiss her awake. He'd forgotten the alarm, just as he'd been the one who'd thought to cancel Saturday's breakfast meeting.

If Sam wanted to spend today with him, she was going to have to suggest it.

That's stupid, Karas.

The voice inside him had spoken with amusement that bordered on contempt but he'd ignored it, eased his arm from beneath Sam's head, risen from the bed and turned off the alarm clock. And, just as he'd known she would, when she awoke her first thought had been of her job and not of him.

Hell. Demetrios frowned into his coffee cup. He was not only being stupid, he was being childish. If he wanted them to skip today's meeting, all he had to do was say so. He was her employer. Maybe she was waiting for him to make the decision. For all he knew she'd smile, open her arms and say she'd been hoping he'd say something like that.

He smiled, dumped his cup in the sink, tugged at his tie, started for the stairs...and saw Sam, coming down them, clutching the banister with one hand and the cane in the other.

"What are you doing?" he demanded.

It was a foolish question. He knew the answer. She wasn't just disdaining his assistance, she was hell-bent on going to work. So much for telling her he'd decided they should stay home, and for her greeting the news with a smile.

Anger raged through him.

"You are impossible," he snapped. "Didn't I tell you to call me? You can't be trusted to use your head!"

"You mean, I can't be trusted to let you take over my life," she retorted.

He stared at her. She stared at him. Then he cursed, ran up the stairs, took her in his arms and they shared a kiss that almost turned him inside out.

"We don't have to go to the office today," he whispered.

"I thought that was what you wanted to do."

"You're the one who reminded me to set the alarm."

"Only so you could tell me that you didn't want to set it."

He smiled. She smiled, too.

"We're all dressed," he said softly. "I suppose we could go to the office for a while."

"We could take a long lunch."

"We could work only half a day."

"Agreed. But until then, we'll be models of decorum."

He smiled. "Of course."

It surprised her when he kept his word. Though he carried her to the helicopter and then to his car, turning aside his driver's offer of help, he stood by politely when they pulled up at Karas Lines, only offering his hand to her for support. But she saw his jaw tighten when they reached the steps that led to the conference room.

"Sam," he said in a low, warning voice.

Her grim look was all the caution he needed. Step by step, she made her way to the top. She was panting a little when she got there but she flashed him a quick, triumphant grin.

"You see, Mr. Karas?" she said. "I'm perfectly capable of taking care of myself."

She was, and he wasn't sure if that was good or bad. He loved her spirit but he loved taking care of her. His feelings for her were complex. *She* was complex. He watched as she hobbled into the conference room and thought that he could spend the rest of his life being fascinated by her and then he thought, *the rest of my life?*

What kind of idea was that?

The damned Frenchman and the impossible Italian shot to their feet as Sam made her way through the door, both of them demanding to know what had happened and what they could do to help.

"I had a little accident," Sam said pleasantly. "Thank you both, but I'm fine."

"Nonsense," the Frenchman said. "You will require assistance."

"If she does," Demetrios said abruptly, "I will provide it." Everyone looked at him and he saw Sam's eyes narrow. "I am her employer," he said, as if that explained everything.

The meeting began. She was back to addressing him formally. He'd expected it, knew it was actually a good idea not to let the others know they'd become involved. Still, it grated on him whenever she called him Mr. Karas, although not as badly as it did whenever the Frenchman or the Italian stopped the discussion to ask if she wanted water or coffee or anything at all.

But he kept his temper. In fact, he was congratulating himself on it when suddenly the Italian translator said she was sorry, but if they could just take a five minute break while she checked something?

"Of course," Demetrios said. He took a quick look at his watch. It was almost noon. Almost time to tell everyone that they were done for the day. Then he could get out of this place with Sam. Maybe she'd like to fly to Kythira. He knew a wonderful little inn with a great restaurant and a private white sand beach, so private she wouldn't need that bikini.

The little group pushed back their chairs. He watched Sam clutch the armrest as she worked out the easiest way to get to her feet. He knew the easiest way would be to let him lift her into his arms but he also knew she would go crazy if he did…and then the Frenchman rushed to her side.

"Let me assist you, *mademoiselle*," he said, and slid an arm around her shoulders.

Demetrios moved before he thought. "I am all the assistance she needs," he growled, jostling the other man aside and doing what he'd promised himself he would not do, putting his arm around Sam in a gesture so protective and obvious that he knew he'd given the game away to everyone in that room…

And knew, as well, that he'd fallen in love with her.

They flew to Kythira, lay on the beach, ate shrimp and drank white wine and made love in the sun.

Demetrios tried not to think about that sudden revelation he'd had in the office, but he couldn't get it out of his head. Maybe that was why it took him a while to realize something was wrong.

Sam was quiet. Too quiet.

She was quiet that night, too, when they dined on the patio. The cook had outdone herself. Tall white tapers burned in silver holders; flowers spilled from a silver basket in the center of the table and a bottle of white wine stood chilling near at hand.

But something was wrong. Demetrios knew it. It had nothing to do with what had happened at the office. Yes, people had shuffled their feet, stammered flimsy excuses and left after his little outburst, but he and Sam had dealt with it. Alone in the conference room, she'd told him precisely what she thought of the way he'd made their relationship public. He'd apologized and she'd sighed, gone into his arms and kissed him even though anyone could have walked in.

He'd taken that as a good sign but now she was so silent...

Yes, something was wrong. What was it? And what was he doing, sitting and watching her for signs? He was afraid to ask her what was going on. He, Demetrios Karas, afraid to ask a woman why she was so quiet, why she'd stopped smiling and had taken, instead, to shooting him little looks he could not read.

The maid wheeled a serving cart out the door and left it beside the table. Sam ignored it, so he fixed a plate for her, then for himself. The food looked appetizing, but he had no desire to eat. He pushed things from one side of the plate to the other. Sam didn't even make the attempt. Just those little looks...

"Dammit," he roared, tossing his napkin on the table, "what's the matter?"

He hadn't intended to say that. He'd planned on keeping still, or perhaps asking, gently, if something was troubling her. But he couldn't handle this. He was still trying to come to grips with the shock of falling in love with Sam and she was treating him like a leper.

"I'm sorry," he said, far more calmly. "But you must tell me what's going on, Sam. I'm not good at reading tea leaves."

Sam looked up from her glass of wine. It was a delicious wine but she'd had hardly any of it. She was filled with despair.

This long, lovely, wonderful day had made her see just how much trouble she was in.

The simple truth was that she'd never actually been in a relationship before. She hadn't know that, until now, but dating a man, liking him, sleeping with him didn't really constitute a relationship, even if it lasted for weeks or months.

This—this quagmire she'd stumbled into with Demetrios was a relationship with a capital R, the sort of thing that made her want to weep and laugh at the same time. He walked into a room, and she grew dizzy with pleasure. He all but announced to the world that she belonged to him, and she had to pretend she was angry because in her heart— in her heart, she wanted to shout it from the rooftops, that she was his and he was hers...

And she loved him.

And what a time to realize it, standing in a conference room, addressing Demetrios as Mr. Karas, watching him glower...but then, she had never done anything in the conventional way. Why would she fall in love like anybody else, with violins and moonlight—and a man who would love her in return?

Demetrios never would.

She'd known all that in a heartbeat this morning, puzzled over what to do about it for the remainder of the day, and she still had no answer. It didn't help that he was glaring at her, his eyes snapping with anger despite his stilted apology. As if he had anything to be angry about, the unfeeling idiot.

"Did you hear me?" he said. "I'm sorry I yelled."

"I heard you."

"Sam, dammit..." He took a breath. "Are you angry? That thing this morning..."

"I'm not angry," she said softly. "But—but I have to say some things that—that aren't easy."

"What things?" he said, while a chasm opened at his feet.

She swallowed dryly, moistened her lips, looked anywhere but at him. "I've been wondering if—if maybe we went into this too quickly."

"Into what?"

His voice was soft. She had come to know that softness. It hid a rock-hard determination but she was determined, too. It was time to decide how to progress, *if* to progress, whether to stay with Demetrios until the inevitable end or walk away now.

She didn't know which way would be the best, even after spending most of the day thinking about it. Pain now, or pain later? It was an impossible decision. She'd always found relationships so easy to handle. Amanda had talked a little about how tortured she'd been, trying to figure out what she felt for Nick; Carin had sworn how much she despised Rafe to anyone who'd listen, and Sam had just taken it all in and wondered how a woman could possibly become so confused in her dealings with a man.

She owed her sisters an apology.

"You wonder if we went into what too quickly?" Demetrios said, and she looked at him.

If sleeping with your boss was a mistake, falling in love with him was sheer disaster. Of course, she wouldn't tell him that. She'd say that she'd decided she realized she couldn't give up the loss of independence that would go with being intimately involved with him, that it had been a mistake to let the relationship become personal.

"Into this—this—"

"We are lovers." He spoke curtly. "Is that so difficult to acknowledge?"

"No. It's not. What I mean is… Don't look at me like that!"

"Like what?" he said, and told himself that if he'd been required to pay a *drachma* for every time he'd wanted to shake this woman since he'd met her, he'd be well on his way to the poorhouse by now.

Sam shoved back her chair and got to her feet. "Don't!" she said, as he sprang up, too. "I am perfectly capable of moving around on my own. I sprained my ankle, Demetrios, I didn't break it."

"Ah."

"Ah, what? Must you always sound so smug?"

"I was right," he said calmly. He could be calm, now

that he knew the problem. For a few seconds, he'd thought she was about to tell him she'd decided against their affair. Their relationship. Whatever in hell you called it when a man fell in love with a woman who didn't love him, a woman he didn't want to be in love with.

But that was ridiculous. Samantha enjoyed being with him. She enjoyed what happened in bed. All she needed was a little reassurance that he would respect her independence. Well, he could manage that. He just had to back off a little, convince her that all he wanted from her was what they already had.

It wasn't even a lie.

Try as he might, he had no idea exactly what he *did* want. Marriage? Children? From what he knew of such things, he wasn't exactly desirous of them. He would tell her that, let her see that she risked nothing by continuing their affair.

And, over the weeks and months that came next, if he changed his mind, well, then he would set out to change hers. If he didn't...if he didn't, that would be that.

It was a logical solution. He felt better for having reached it, and he smiled as he walked towards her.

"Sam, *kalóz mou*..." To his surprise, she slapped at his hands when he tried to clasp her shoulders.

"I just don't..." Her throat tightened. What was wrong with her? Was she going to cry because he called her his beloved without meaning it? "I want to say what I need to say, all right? Without you stopping me."

"But it isn't necessary."

"God give me strength! You're impossible, Demetrios! You always think you know what's necessary. Well, I have news for you. You don't. "

"Sweetheart," he said with total sincerity, "I understand what's troubling you."

Sam folded her arms. "In that case, tell me. Go ahead. Read my mind."

"You are concerned that I'm taking over your life."

"It's a lot more complicated than that."

"Mostly, you are afraid I may want too much from you."

How could a man be so wrong? "Really," she said dryly.

"But I don't. I won't." He put his arm around her. She didn't melt into him, as she would have last night, even this afternoon, but she let him do it. He took that as a good omen. "I understand how difficult it is for a woman like you to have an affair with a man like me."

"Of course you do. You know everything."

He decided to let that pass. "My mother was American. Did you know that?"

"Maybe. Amanda might have said..." Sam puffed out a breath. "You're not going to divert me by talking about your mother."

"She was a singer. A coloratura. Do you know what...?"

"Yes," she said impatiently, "of course I do. It's a soprano with an exceptionally light, clear voice."

"That's right." He tugged her down beside him on a wicker love seat. "She was a good woman, but she and my father should never have gotten married."

Sam stared at him. "What?"

"She was like you," he said, bringing her hand to his lips. "Beautiful. Fiercely independent. Argumentative. Difficult."

"I am neither argumentative nor difficult."

He smiled. "And my father...well, I suppose I am very much like him."

"Conceited. Impossible. Authoritative."

"I am Greek," he said, as if that explained everything. "Well, half-Greek, but it is the same thing. He was the one who raised me."

Sam had promised herself she wouldn't let him drag her down this detour but not asking the inevitable question was impossible.

"Why? What happened to your mother?"

His smile dimmed. "She'd become restless. She missed her country, her friends, her career..." He caught himself in midsentence. This was not what he'd wanted to tell her.

His father had explained what had driven his parents apart, but that was not the point. "They quarreled often. She would leave, fly to New York. He would go after her and bring her back. And then, one day, he didn't go after her. She stayed in America and he stayed here."

"I don't understand. Didn't you grow up in Greece?"

"Yes."

"But you just said your mother went back to the States."

"I didn't go with her. My father would not permit it."

"He would not...?" Sam stared at him, at that imperious face that no longer bore a smile but had, instead, taken on the stoniness of marble. "She let him get away with that?"

"Sam. You must try and understand. This is Greece. The rules are different here. A man is still the head of his household in my country."

"What you mean is, your father could keep you despite your mother's wishes."

"Yes. No." Demetrios frowned and got to his feet. The conversation was not going at all as he'd planned. "She didn't mind. She loved me, in her way, but she was not a woman whose maternal instincts ran deep. Do you understand?"

"No. I don't. If I had a child, I could never let anything keep me from it."

"The law was on my father's side. Would you expect a man to give up his own flesh and blood?"

"There's such a thing as joint custody. In America—"

"I tell you again, this is Greece. Besides, why would anyone wish a child to be batted back and forth across the Atlantic, like a ball at a tennis match?" He hadn't intended to say that, either. What did such things matter, after all these years? "This is all beside the point, Samantha. What you should understand is—"

"What happened?" Sam asked softly. "To your parents' marriage?"

"They were divorced."

"And where is your mother now? I know your father died

a few years ago but I don't think I ever heard anything about your mother.''

"She is still alive," he said stiffly. "She lives in Argentina with a man who raises horses.''

"She moved there after the divorce?''

"She moved there,'' he said coldly, "when I was thirteen. By then, she'd been living in New York for five years. And, before you ask, until she left the States I saw her for two weeks each July, when my father permitted her—''

"Permitted her?'' Sam said, incredulously.

"That's right. He allowed her to come to Athens and stay in an apartment he owned, and spend whatever time she wished with me.''

Sam stood up and put her hand on his arm. The muscles were taut beneath her fingers.

"That's terrible,'' she said softly. "Demetrios, I'm so sorry…''

"Don't be.'' He shook off her hand and looked at her, his eyes cold. "It was all she was entitled to. She was the wrong woman for my father, not the kind a man should take as a wife or wish to be the mother of his child.''

Sam drew back. "You don't know that. You don't know the whole story. Maybe there's more to it.''

"People marry for the wrong reasons, Samantha. For passion. For sex. They call it love, but it isn't.'' He reached out for her, his hands cruel on her shoulders. Why had it seemed so confusing, just a little while ago? He knew what he wanted and it wasn't love or marriage or fatherhood. "And that is why you have nothing to fear from me. I won't demand anything but what you can give because it's all I want.''

Nothing to fear? She wanted to laugh. He thought he knew her. The worst of it was, she'd thought she knew herself but in the blink of an eye, she'd gone from wanting to go through life without leaving footprints to wanting to build a safe, warm nest where she could do all the mundane things other women did, like wake up in the morning in the arms of the man she loved and, some day, soothe the bruised knees of little boys who were tiny replicas of their father.

How could she have fallen so hard, so fast?

"Sam?" He slid his hands from her shoulders to her face, lifted it to his. "You mean more to me than a woman ever has. You're beautiful. You're exciting. You make me happy. And I please you. I know that I do."

She wanted to tear free and run. Her heart was pounding. But she stood still, even managed to choke out a laugh.

"Such modesty, Demetrios."

"I'm being honest. You must do the same. We aren't dreamers in need of fairy tale endings."

"No." Her voice shook. "No, we're not."

"I will give you everything, *matyá mou*. Not only honesty but respect. I will pledge you my fidelity for as long as we are together, but I won't tell you lies—and I will not expect any from you. Do you understand?"

He fell silent, hearing only the sound of his own hammering pulse. He had not planned to say any of this, had not even known it was inside him, but he was glad it had come out. It was all the truth and whatever he'd imagined about falling in love with Samantha had been sentimental self-deceit.

He was his father's son but he would not be the fool his father had been, and certainly she could understand that. He would not ask for what she could not give. He would never expect her to love him to the exclusion of anything else, or to take vows she would not keep, or to bear his child.

He could see her mouth trembling. Had he hurt her? For a second, he almost pulled her into his arms to say it wasn't true, that he loved her, would always love her, that she had only to say that she loved him...

"I was going to tell you that I was leaving you," she said in a low voice.

"But now you won't."

Sam stared up into the face of this man she loved, this man she'd been determined to leave, and saw not the man but the child he had once been, abandoned by a mother who had not loved him.

"Sam." He took her face in his hands. "Stay with me."

He kissed her, and she put her arms around him and kissed him back, trying not to weep, weeping anyway—and not knowing if the tears were for him or for herself. All she knew was that the anguish she felt now was nothing compared to what she would feel when he tired of her.

Then she would pay for this night's decision with a broken heart.

CHAPTER TEN

FOR the next few weeks, Sam was blissfully happy.

Demetrios was an incredible lover. She'd never known a man quite like him. He was fun, he was exciting, he was thoughtful and caring. Just when she thought she'd figured him out, he'd surprise her. He stopped the car to buy her a single rose from a street vendor; he spirited her to Florence for a weekend and bought her a tiny gold charm in the shape of a kitten with emerald eyes because, he said, it reminded him of her. Like her, he got as much pleasure out of spending the evening home as he did from going out.

And when they were alone and in each other's arms, he made her forget the world and everything in it.

They never talked about the future.

That should have been fine. Sam had always liked living that way. There was a kick in not knowing what you'd be doing a month from now, whether you'd be working in a thatched hut or in a suite at the Georges V. Life wasn't supposed to be a road map you could read. Living from day to day was far more exciting than having a master plan.

If you knew too much about the future, things would grow dull.

That was what Sam had always thought. Now, she discovered that it wasn't true.

She loved knowing she'd go to sleep in Demetrios's arms and wake to his kisses. She adored the sweet predictability of knowing they'd have their first cups of coffee while he shaved and she put on her makeup, that at night they'd talk over the day's events, that curling up together to read or watch a movie on the VCR made her every bit as content as going out to a party. More content, maybe, because being alone with him was wonderful.

The only danger was her fear that one of those nights she'd turn to him and blurt out the truth, that she loved him more each day.

Sam knew she must never do anything so foolish.

Demetrios had been brutally honest. He'd told her how he felt about love and what he expected of her, and those expectations surely didn't include finding himself with a lovestruck woman on his hands. There was a world of difference between being a man's lover and his beloved.

Or in being his mistress.

The funny thing was that she'd never thought of herself as his mistress until one night, when he took her to the opening of a new restaurant.

"I don't really want to go," he said, as they drove along a narrow, twisting road on the rocky hillside overlooking Athens, "but an old friend owns the place. We won't stay long, sweetheart."

"Don't be silly," Sam said. "We'll stay as long as you like. It'll be fun."

It was, until Demetrios stepped away for a moment and a stunning blonde wearing a dress that left nothing to the imagination wandered up to Sam.

"How nice to finally get a look at you," she'd said in a throaty purr.

Sam had offered a puzzled smile. "Sorry?"

"Some of us have been wondering what you look like," the blonde said. "You *are* Demetrios's new mistress, aren't you?"

Demetrios had come back just then, put his arm around Sam's waist, introduced her to the blonde in a way that made it clear, at least, that there'd never been anything between them. The blonde wandered off and Sam got through the evening even though she felt as if everyone was watching her and talking about her. She'd never told Demetrios what had happened, but she couldn't forget it—and yet, it was true. That was what she was, wasn't she? His mistress?

She lived with him. He paid for the roof over her head and the food she ate; he wanted to do more than that, to buy her clothes and jewels. She wouldn't let him, but that didn't change the facts. She was his mistress.

The word itself had an old-fashioned feel to it, probably a certain sexy charm in the circles in which he moved. It had a less exalted meaning in Sam's world. Well, so what? She'd never given a damn for convention. People could call her what they wished. What did words matter, when two people belonged together?

A lot, or so it seemed.

The answer she'd come up with, that all that counted was that she belonged with Demetrios and he belonged with her, began to seem more and more facile as the four months she'd agreed to work for him rushed towards their inevitable conclusion. Mistresses, by definition, lived uncertain lives. A mistress never knew where she'd be or what man she'd be with next year or even next month, and Sam knew exactly where she wanted to be. She'd found a man, *the* man, who was the other half of her.

Sometimes, in the late hours of the night, she'd lie in his arms after they made love and think how amazing it was that she'd never even known she was searching for him…and wonder when she was going to lose him. The role of mistress came with a beginning and an end. You didn't have to be a genius to understand that—and if she was foolish enough to harbor any doubts, she had only to recall how bluntly Demetrios had told her he'd had other mistresses before her.

She might be the only one he'd ever asked to live with him, but that didn't change the basics. There had been women before her; there would be women after her. It was a simple fact of life—and the more she tried not to dwell on it, the more she did.

She began noticing a change in him, too. Was it her imagination, or was he treating her differently? Was he more formal? More removed? Did he spend more time in his study at night and less with her?

As the days passed, she could hardly think about anything else. It didn't help that she wasn't feeling well. A nasty flu had gone around Piraeus and Athens; for weeks, people had coughed and sneezed and been nauseous. Everyone was over it—everyone but Sam.

Her body felt heavy; she was tired all the time. Her stomach did a delicate dance, especially in the mornings. Or maybe it wasn't flu. Maybe she was already reacting to what was going to happen in less than two weeks, when her term of employment ended.

She was going to leave Greece, and Demetrios. Her job was ending, and so would their affair.

By the last week of her contract, all the parties had agreed to the deal in principle. The lawyers would step in now and put things in language that would be binding. On Friday, Sam sat in the conference room at Karas Lines, listening to the buzz of conversation around her, trying to concentrate on her job—and failing miserably.

For days, she'd waited for Demetrios to talk about what would happen when the contracts were signed. In moments of painful honesty, she knew that she'd waited for him to ask her to stay with him.

He hadn't.

For the thousandth time, she told herself it was for the best. It eliminated lots of problems. She couldn't have said yes, even if he'd asked her. She had a life in the States. She had a career. She couldn't just give it all up and go on being his mistress—could she?

Sam looked down at her notepad, stared blindly at the scribbled words. How could she, of all women, have been reduced to this? She was waiting for a man to ask her a question that would decide her future. No. This was impossible. She couldn't have put herself in such a humiliating position.

"…doesn't seem possible, does it?"

She blinked, looked up. The Italian translator was leaning in close, obviously waiting for an answer to whatever question she'd asked. The formal meeting had ended, though Sam had never noticed. Demetrios and the others had risen from their chairs; they stood in a loose circle, the Frenchman and the Italian chatting…

The hair rose on the back of her neck. Demetrios was staring at her, his eyes as cold as she'd ever seen them.

Sam forced herself to look at her Italian counterpart. "Sorry," she said, "I missed that."

"I said it seems hard to believe this is almost over and I'll be in Rome in a few days." The woman frowned. "Samantha? Are you all right?"

Did her despair show on her face? That would be the ultimate humiliation.

"I'm fine," Sam said quickly, "just a little tired." She reached for her briefcase, opened it and began putting her pads and pencils away. "I think I'm coming down with that flu that was going around."

"Better late than never," the woman said, smiling, "although 'never' is probably the best time to come down with a bug. Here's hoping you're over it before you fly home." She paused. "Or were you planning to stay on for a while?"

The other translator's smile was bland but her eyes were bright with questions. It was easy to see what she was thinking. For months, Demetrios had given Sam private little smiles. Those smiles had all but vanished. Sam had been painfully aware of it but she hadn't considered the others might have noticed. Now she knew that they had, that they might even have whispered about it behind her back.

She jammed another few pieces of paper into the briefcase and snapped the clasp shut. "I'm not sure," she said briskly. "I'm still trying to decide what to do next."

Damn you, Demetrios, she thought. *Damn you for doing this to me!*

And yet, she couldn't blame it all on him. If he held such

power over her, she'd given it to him. She'd never been stupid enough to put herself in a man's hands before. She'd run her own life, made her own rules, and gone from that to all but groveling to a man who hardly noticed her anymore, except in bed—and not even there lately.

When had that happened? When had he stopped turning to her the last thing at night and the first thing in the morning? He still made love to her but it wasn't the same. She could feel him holding something back and it hurt, so much so that she felt herself holding back, too.

She didn't come up behind him when he was shaving anymore, slip her arms around him and touch him the way she once had. In the beginning, she'd been completely uninhibited with him. Not anymore. She'd turn into his arms, reach for him—and wonder, suddenly, if he were only accommodating her, if his response to her was only of the body and not of the heart.

What heart? That part of his anatomy had never been involved in what went on between them.

Sam felt herself tremble with barely suppressed anger. At Demetrios. At herself. She wanted to fly across the room and beat her fists against his chest. Even if she did, what would be the point? Nothing would change. He didn't love her. He never had and he never would.

She shoved back her chair and rose to her feet. Her vision blurred; the room grayed. She put out a hand, clasped the table edge for support.

"Mademoiselle? Are you ill?"

Sam took a shuddering breath. "I'm okay." She shook her head, cleared her vision and smiled shakily at the Frenchman. "Well, maybe not. I seem to be coming down with the flu."

"So late in the season?" The Frenchman's eyes narrowed. "Why not let me help you to that little settee in *Monsieur* Karas's private office? You can lie down, put your feet up—"

"If Miss Brewster needs help," Demetrios said, "I will

provide it.'' Hadn't he made the same kind of ridiculous statement once before? he thought furiously, as he shouldered past the Frenchman and put his arm around Sam's waist. Why did he keep making a spectacle of himself over this woman? ''Thank you for your assistance,'' he said, in a tone that made it obvious that wasn't what he meant at all. ''I am here now.''

The Frenchman shot Sam a sympathetic look. ''But of course. *Mademoiselle*, I hope you feel better soon.''

Sam waited until the room cleared. Then she pulled loose of Demetrios's embrace and turned her flushed face up to his.

''That was incredibly rude!''

''What happened to you? Are you ill?''

''I'm getting the flu. He was only trying to help me.''

''Help you?'' Demetrios snorted. ''The man has spent four months trying to get you into bed.''

''That's so ridiculous it doesn't deserve a response.''

''Do you think our relationship grants you the right to treat me with disrespect? To let another man put his hands on you while I watch?''

Sam stared at him. Then she grabbed her briefcase and strode towards the door.

''Samantha? Samantha! Come back here. I did not say you could leave!''

She didn't stop. Demetrios cursed and went after her as she disappeared down the hall. He could feel the adrenaline coursing through his veins like a river in flood. He'd been angry with her for days. Angry? Hell, he'd been furious. How dare she treat him as she'd been doing? The silence. The moodiness. The way she got into bed at night and turned her back to him.

Now she'd made him look like a fool. Why had he ever gotten involved with a woman who didn't know her place?

He caught her at the foot of the steps and wrapped his hand around her wrist.

"Are you deaf?" he snarled. "Didn't you hear what I said?"

"I heard you." Sam glared at him. "If you think we're going back to the days of sit, stay and heel, you can think again."

"Crazy, as well as deaf. What the hell are you talking about?"

"Let go of me."

"I will, when you start to make sense." He narrowed his eyes at her. "Something is wrong with you lately."

"You're what's wrong with me," she snapped. "And I'm tired of putting up with it."

A muscle knotted in his cheek. "This is hardly the place for such a discussion. What I wish to say to you should be said in privacy."

Sam wanted to weep. Instead, she lifted her chin. "This is private enough."

"A doorway in my office building is hardly private." His hand closed on her elbow. Grimly, he marched her out to the street and to his car. He had taken the Ferrari today and he held on to her while he unlocked the door. "Get in."

"Do you ever say 'please'?"

"Not often, no. Get in, dammit—or did you intend to wander the streets alone? Perhaps you've forgotten what happened the last time you did that."

"Oh, I remember, all right." Tears burned in her eyes but she'd sooner have died than let them flow. It was bad enough he thought he could treat her this way, go from days of indifference to out and out hostility. She would never let him steal what little remained of her pride. "How could I forget when I've wished that night, and everything that came after it, never happened?"

Demetrios stared at her, his eyes cold and flat. "Get in the car," he said softly.

What would she gain by not complying? Sam pulled free of his hand and got into the Ferrari. They didn't exchange a word all the way to the heliport, or to Astra.

The house was unusually quiet. Cosimia was away on a long weekend and it was the cook's day off. Sam had forgotten that, just as she'd forgotten how much she'd foolishly looked forward to being completely alone with Demetrios. She'd imagined puttering in the kitchen, cooking for him, making him scrambled eggs and cheese the way she had late one night. He'd acted as if he'd never eaten anything better. Ambrosia, he'd said, fit for the gods, and then he'd kissed her.

Now, she wished Cosimia were present, if only to break the heavy silence.

Demetrios took off his suit jacket and tossed it on a chair. His tie went next. Then he undid the top buttons of his shirt and rolled up his sleeves. It was a break from routine. Normally, they went upstairs, showered together. Sometimes, an hour or more slipped by before they thought about anything but each other.

"I'm going to have a drink." He walked past her to his study. "Scotch, on the rocks. Do you want one?"

That, too, was different. She'd never seen him drink anything but wine.

"No," she said carefully, "I don't."

Demetrios went to the breakfront and poured an inch of whiskey into a Baccarat tumbler, and knew right away that he'd made a mistake. He was in no hurry to have this talk with Samantha. Wine would have made a better diversion. Choosing a bottle, uncorking it, pouring it would all have taken time. On the other hand, wine would not numb his growing anger, once the discussion ended.

Discussion? That was an amazing word to use for a conversation he was certain would leave him empty.

Demetrios looked at the tumbler of Scotch. To hell with it, he thought, and tossed the whiskey down his throat, let it burn its fiery way into his belly, but it did nothing to dispel the chill that had been with him for days now, for weeks, ever since he'd realized the days were rushing past and Samantha clearly didn't give a damn that their time together was ending.

He reached for the bottle and thought better of it. There was a delicate balance between the amount of alcohol a man needed to calm him and the amount it took to make his temper explode. He concentrated instead on how he'd felt when he saw the Frenchman standing with his arm curved protectively around Sam's shoulders, his face a study in false concern, and the way she'd been looking at him, as if he were Lancelot and she Queen Guinevere.

Demetrios put down the tumbler, took a few seconds to compose himself, and turned to the woman who had shared his bed and his life the past three months. She was standing just inside the door to the study, her posture stiff with removal. Her face was pale and her eyes blazed with anger, though for one incredibly foolish minute, he almost thought that what he saw glittering in her eyes were tears.

She was so beautiful. More beautiful than ever, if that were possible. She had changed, in some subtle way he couldn't put his finger on. Her body seemed more lush, her breasts still small but with a new roundness, her belly gently convex. Perhaps it was simply that he noticed things differently, now that she'd stopped offering herself to him with such heart-stopping eagerness.

When he made love to her lately, it was he who did the asking with a touch, a kiss, a whisper, and even though she still responded, he knew she held back. That killed him. She had never held anything back, not at the beginning. She'd been open to whatever they did in bed, open to life with an infectious joy that had made him feel renewed. He had never known a woman like her. She could weep at *Aida* and laugh at a children's cartoon. She could take as much joy in a seashell as in a jewel, and kiss him with tenderness as well as passion.

Most of all, he'd never known a woman who could make him forget the world and want only her.

How could she leave him, without so much as a backward glance?

He'd never considered what would happen when her four month contract ended. Why should he? Surely, she'd want to stay with him. That was what he'd assumed.

How could he have been so damn stupid?

What they'd had was only an interlude in her pursuit of freedom. She was ready to move on. He could tell by the way she behaved. She was withdrawing from the life they shared, and there was nothing he could do about it except beg her to tell him why she wanted to leave him...and he'd sooner have suffered the tortures of Tantalus than do something as stupid as that.

Hell, he thought, and turned back to the whiskey and poured another inch in the glass.

Why was he being so maudlin? How long could an affair last? Maybe the trouble was that he'd let Samantha get the upper hand. He should be the one who was ending things, not she.

He put down the whiskey and turned towards her again. "Samantha..."

She shook her head, silenced him with an upheld hand. "You don't have to say it." Her voice was husky. "I know."

"It's over," he said flatly.

"Yes. It is."

"You are eager to return to your own life."

He was putting words into her mouth. Was he being gallant, or was he only hoping to avoid a scene? He didn't have to worry. She'd sooner have died than let him know the truth.

"Yes."

He cleared his throat. "When will you leave?"

Did he want her gone right away? "Next week. When my contract ends."

"There's no rush. I mean, if you wanted to stay on for a while..."

He could afford to be polite, now that she'd said she was leaving. For the second time that day, she wanted to strike him.

"Thank you," she said, and managed to smile. "But I think it would be better, all around, if I left next week just as we'd planned. I have—I have some interviews lined up."

A hot throb of anger beat in his blood. He could feel his composure slipping. As they'd planned? They had *planned* no such thing. They had never talked of when she would leave him, but it was obvious she had thought about it. She'd even arranged for job interviews. All the times he'd been holding her, trying to figure out how he'd lived without her in his life, she'd been thinking ahead, arranging her future—a future that didn't involve him.

"Really," he said, very calmly. "You have job interviews lined up?"

She nodded. It was a lie, but she needed to cloak herself in falsehoods if she were going to get through this.

"Well, one or two."

He narrowed his eyes. "You are going to work for the Frenchman."

"For God's sake, Demetrios—" Sam took a breath. "No. Not for him. I, uh, I sent out some e-mails a couple of weeks ago."

"A couple of weeks ago," he said softly, ominously. "While you were still in my—in my employ."

"Well, yes." She forced a laugh. "But I did it on my own time."

"Your time belongs to me. All of it." He came towards her; she took a step back. "Until the day you walk out of this house, you are mine."

"Do you have any idea how silly that sounds?" She wanted to try another laugh but she was afraid it would come out a sob. "You don't own me."

"I have owned you for the past three months," he said roughly. He reached for her, pulled her into his arms. "You have been mine."

"That might play well in your country, Demetrios, but not—"

He cupped her face and crushed her mouth beneath his. Sam told herself she wouldn't let this happen. It was over. What had existed between them was done...but she felt the race of his heart against hers, the hardness of his erect flesh against her belly, and knew that she would take this one last night before leaving him.

She put her arms around him and kissed him back. He lifted her and carried her up the stairs to his bedroom, undressed her slowly, savoring the taste of her mouth, her skin, the nectar that he sought out and found between her thighs. When he entered her, it was with a slowness that almost killed him, but he wanted all of it, all of her, to see the darkness fill her eyes, the color flood her face, to hear the sounds she made, the whispers and sighs that told him how much she wanted him here, if no place else.

"Look at me," he demanded, when he knew she was nearing climax. He caught her hands, linked their fingers together. "Look at me," he said again, and when she did he pressed deep inside her, pulled back, rocked into her again and again until she was frantic, bucking against him, begging him for release. "Now," he whispered, and she convulsed around him as he let go of everything that anchored him to the world and lost himself in this woman who had changed him, forever.

He buried his face in her throat, absorbing her smell, her shudders. Once, he'd always held her like this, after they made love; lately, he'd used every excuse not to, but the time for excuses was over. With Sam in his arms, with their flesh still joined, he knew he'd left her because he was afraid to stay with her, afraid to look into himself and face what she had come to mean to him.

Was it possible she cared for him? That she was only waiting for some sign? He took a deep breath, rolled to his side and scooped her against him. "Sam," he said softly, "kitten..."

She was asleep. That was just as well. He wasn't sure of what he really wanted to tell her. Perhaps it would be clear, in the morning.

But when he awoke, she was gone. All she'd left behind was a note that said she hadn't known how to tell him that she'd already accepted one of those job offers. She thought it best if she left now, instead of next week. The deal was concluded. He didn't actually need her services anymore.

He felt himself turn hot with fury. He shot from the bed, pulled on his clothes and went after his helicopter pilot. White-faced, the man said Miss Brewster had requested transport to the Athens airport. Was there a reason he should have turned her down?

Demetrios stared at the pilot. "No," he said, after a moment, "none."

Samantha was gone. The night in his arms had meant nothing to her. And, now that he thought about it, it hadn't meant anything to him, either. Whatever stupid, sentimental crap had oozed through his veins had been the result of good whiskey and good sex, and the world was full of bottles and women who could provide the same thing.

He smiled at the pilot. Women were unpredictable creatures, he said, and clapped the man on the back. Then he returned to the house, dug out the address book he had not looked at since the night he'd first set eyes on Samantha, and placed a call to a brunette in London. He woke her— it was very early in the morning—but she squealed with delight when she heard his voice.

They made plans for what was surely going to be a memorable weekend.

Hours later, as Demetrios was en route to England, a worried housekeeper in Texas awoke Marta Brewster Baron with a soft knock on the bedroom door and then a whisper.

"Thank you, Carmen," Marta said. She threw on a robe and hurried down to the big kitchen of the Texas mansion known as Espada. "Sam?" she said to the trembling young woman seated at the kitchen table.

Sam looked up. "Mom," she said shakily. "I should have phoned first, but—"

"No, no, darling, don't be silly." Marta sat down next to her daughter and gently clasped her hand. "What's happened, sweetie? Are you all right? I thought you were supposed to be in Greece until—"

Sam shot to her feet. "Oh God," she said, and raced to the powder room down the hall.

Marta rose and hurried after her. "Make some tea," she called back to Carmen.

Sam was bent over the toilet. Marta held her shoulders while she retched. When the spasms ended, she sat Sam down on the closed commode and sponged her face with cool water while she took in what had just happened, combined it with the subtle changes she saw in her daughter's face and body and with the experience that came with years of living.

Marta knelt down and took Sam's icy hands in hers.

"Sam, darling," she said, very gently, "when were you going to let us know that you were pregnant?"

CHAPTER ELEVEN

"Pregnant?" Sam said. "Me?"

"You," Marta said gently.

Sam came as close as she could to laughing. "No. Don't be silly. I have the flu. Half the population of Athens had it. I haven't felt well for days…" She caught herself, heard what she saying and felt as if she were suddenly standing on the top of a cliff. "I'm not," she said emphatically. "It's the flu. And the long flight. And—and—"

She began to weep. Marta put an arm around her. "Do you want to talk about it?" she asked softly.

Sam shook her head. "There's nothing to talk about."

"Not even the name of your baby's father?"

"I told you, I'm not pregnant. And even if I were—which I'm not—I wouldn't want him to know. I hate him, Mom. I despise him. I—"

Sam put her face in her hands and begin to cry in earnest. Marta murmured words of comfort, took her upstairs and put her to bed. Then she returned to the kitchen and sipped the tea Carmen had brewed while she tried to decide what troubled her most, that her daughter was unmarried and pregnant or that the determinedly independent child who'd grown into an impossibly independent woman, had come home.

Marta would be forever grateful that she had, but that didn't change the facts. That Sam should have felt desperate enough to come home wasn't just upsetting, it was frightening.

The next morning, Sam borrowed Marta's car, drove into town and bought a home pregnancy test kit.

A waste of time, she kept telling herself. There wasn't a way in the world she could be pregnant. She took the pill. Besides, wouldn't she know? A woman would certainly know something like that.

A little while later, she stood at the bathroom sink, clutching it for support while she stared at the little stick that said her life was about to turn upside down.

The stick must be wrong. She couldn't be pregnant.

"Sam?"

She spun towards the closed door. "I'll—I'll be right out, Mother."

Quickly, she scooped up the stick, the instructions, the box and dumped everything in the trash basket. She was trembling when she opened the door.

"Are you all right, Sam?"

"I'm fine."

Flushed face. Trembling hands. And, sticking up out of the trash, the edge of a box with the word "Pregnancy" printed across it.

"Well," Marta said brightly, "that's good to know. Sam. I was thinking… Why don't I call my GYN and ask him to take a look at you? I know, it's only the flu. You're probably right. You can glare at me afterwards and say you told me so."

It was ridiculous. The whole thing. The test. Her mother. There was only one way to sort this out. "Go ahead," Sam said. "Make the appointment."

The doctor had a cancelation in an hour. Sam almost balked. She hadn't been prepared to get up on the examining table so soon. On the other hand, the sooner she did, the sooner she'd know how stupid all this was.

"I can't be pregnant," she said as she climbed onto the examining table.

The doctor poked and prodded. "Well," he said with professional good cheer, "I hate to argue with you, young lady, but you are."

Sam sat up. "I'm not," she said sharply.

"About three months, I'd say, but we'll do an ultrasound to make sure. I can have the technician see you right now."

"It would be a waste of time. I absolutely cannot be—"

"Have the ultrasound," Marta said softly. "Then you'll know."

What was there to know? Sam thought stubbornly. But there was no way out; the doctor was already on the phone. Sam went down the hall to another examining room, climbed on the table and stared straight ahead while the technician rubbed gel over her skin, then skimmed a small transducer over her belly.

"Okay," she said, "let's just take a look... There we are. See? Right there, down towards the lower right corner of the screen."

Sam reached for her mother's hand and held it in a white-knuckled death grip.

"I don't see anything."

"Darling?" Marta squeezed her hand. "Look at the screen."

"I told you, I don't..." But she did. A tiny blob of protoplasm. A fetus. And she remembered what she'd fought against remembering, the weekend she and Demetrios had become lovers, when she'd skipped a pill and tried to make up for it by taking an extra the next day.

One missed pill. One little slip. Could your entire life really be changed by something so inconsequential?

Marta chattered nervously until they were halfway back to Espada, then fell silent. Jonas Baron came sauntering down the steps as they pulled up to the house. He was trying his best to look unconcerned but not succeeding.

"How you doin', missy?" he asked gruffly.

Sam looked at her stepfather. "I'm doing fine," she said, and went past him into the house.

Left alone, Jonas and Marta looked at each other.

"Well?" he said.

Marta sighed. "She's three months pregnant."

"I hope you told her she can stay with us as long as she wants."

Mara smiled at her husband. "Thank you."

"Nothin' to thank me for. Girl's like one of my own." His jaw knotted and Marta thought how remarkable it was that her husband could still look so strong, so resolute, so young. "She tell you who did this?"

"No."

"It's that Greek, ain't it? The one she was workin' for."

"She didn't tell me, Jonas."

"Yeah, well, who else could it be? I think what this son of a bitch needs is a talkin' to."

"Darling, I know you mean well—"

"What I mean is business."

"It takes two people to make a baby."

"I only see one of 'em on this ranch."

"Maybe he doesn't know." Jonas gave a snort of disbelief. Marta put her hand on his arm. "It's possible. Sam's in denial. How would she have told him she's carrying his child if she didn't know it herself?"

"That stuff only happens in books," he said, "not—"

"Not what?"

Not in real life, he'd been going to say, but a long-buried memory was struggling to the surface, a memory he wasn't willing to stir up just yet.

"Not very often. Sam's not stupid. She must have known."

"Well, she didn't. Or didn't want to, I'm not sure which." Marta looped her arm through her husband's. Together, they climbed the steps and entered the house. "And she doesn't want him to know. That much is clear."

"That's crazy. The man has to stand up to his responsibilities."

"It's Sam's decision, Jonas."

"But if she loves him—"

"If," Marta said gently, "*if*, darling. This is a new world, remember? There's love. There's sex. And the two don't always go together.''

Jonas sighed. ''So, you're tellin' me it ain't his fault he's not here. Okay. There's always that possibility. But now she knows. We know. Hell, the world's gonna know. It's time he knew, too. A man ought to take responsibility if he has a child.''

Marta lay her head on her husband's shoulder. Considering his own past, the son he'd refused to acknowledge for more than thirty years and now loved with all his heart, she wasn't surprised he'd think that. Actually, she agreed with him. Whoever had made her little girl pregnant should know it. And if he already did and he'd turned his back, then he deserved the whipping Jonas was so ready to deliver.

But there was Sam to consider. Her daughter was a grown woman, entitled to make her own choices even if they were poor ones. She'd yet to say she even wanted her baby.

''Let's give this some time. We'll let Sam think about her situation and we won't do anything impetuous while she does.''

''*Some* time,'' Jonas cautioned. ''Not too much.''

''No,'' Marta said, ''not too much.''

She kissed her husband. He went into his study; she continued up the stairs to the second floor and paused at Sam's door.

''Sam?'' Marta knocked gently. ''Darling, may I come in?'' She waited, then opened the door. The blinds were closed, casting the room in artificial twilight. She could see Sam sitting in a rocker, her legs drawn up under her. ''Darling? Are you okay?''

''That sounds like the beginning of a bad joke,'' Sam said. '''Are you okay?' the doctor said to the woman, and she said, 'Well, Doc, that depends on your definition of okay.'''

''Wouldn't some sun be nice?'' Marta said briskly. She didn't wait for an answer. Instead, she walked from window to window, opening the blinds and letting in the light. "There now. Sweetie, I know this is a shock, but—"

"I never even thought of it," Sam said in a small voice. "Isn't that stupid? When I think back on the last few weeks, I don't know how I missed all the signs. I'd stopped getting my period but I just figured it was the pill. I mean, my periods are light as it is..."

"Darling. You don't have to talk about it, if you don't want to."

"And I was nauseous," Sam said, as if her mother hadn't spoken. "I felt like I was riding an elevator that kept making sudden stops. You know?"

"I know," Marta said, sighing. "I still remember, even after all these years."

"I was moody, too, and tired all the time..." Sam shook her head. "Just like Amanda, when she was pregnant, but I didn't put two and two together." She swallowed. "I guess I didn't want to."

"No. Of course you didn't." Marta hesitated. "Still, you must have known. In the back of your mind, I mean, or you wouldn't have..." She hesitated again. "I'm assuming that's why you left—whoever it is that made you pregnant."

"Maybe, subconsciously. The truth is, I left him be-cause—because..." *Because he was tired of me and my heart was breaking, knowing he didn't really want me any-more.*

"Because?" Marta prompted.

"Because our relationship had run its course," Sam said carefully, "the way relationships always do. Why else would I have left him?"

Why, indeed? A woman who left a man for such a logical reason didn't turn up on her mother's doorstep looking hol-low-eyed with despair, but Marta knew better than to say that.

"And now it turns out I'm pregnant." Sam took a breath. "I just can't believe it. I never intended—"

"Lots of pregnancies begin that way, darling."

"This isn't *lots* of pregnancies, Mother. This is *my* pregnancy." She took a shaky breath. "I never thought about having children."

Marta sat down on the edge of the bed. "I know, baby. As I said, lots of—"

"No." Sam uncurled her legs and leaned forward. "You *don't* know. Maybe I'm not saying it right. I really didn't intend to have kids. Not ever."

"Sam," Marta said carefully, "I've watched you with your nieces and nephews. You're wonderful with children."

"Only because I knew they belonged to someone else," Sam said bluntly. "It's lovely to coo to a baby and cuddle it, even to wipe up after it, when you know you can give it a kiss at the end of the day, hand it over to its mother and go back to your own life."

"I see."

"Do you?"

Marta nodded. "Yes." She took a deep breath. "And I'll support whatever decision you feel you must make, darling."

"Decision?"

"About what—what's happening."

Sam gave a harsh laugh. "I'm pregnant, Mom. You might as well say the word."

"No. I mean, I'd rather not, if you've decided to—to—"

"Decided to…?" Sam stared at her mother. "You think I'm not going through with it," she said softly.

"Samantha, you're my child. I know, I know. You're an adult, you make your own choices but you'll always be my little girl. I'll be there for you, whatever you do. I'd never turn away from you, even if—"

"Mom." Sam reached for her mother's hands and clasped them tightly. "I'm going to have my baby."

Relief shuddered through Marta's heart. "I thought you were saying—"

"What I was saying," Sam said, with a little catch in her voice, "is that I really believed I never wanted kids or any

of the rest of it, for that matter. You know. The house—
puppy—kitten—babies thing. It didn't interest me.''

"And now it does?''

"Amazing, isn't it?'' She gave a choked laugh. "That I'd
suddenly want to trade a—a trip to Morocco for a trip to
the maternity ward?''

Marta smiled. "Not so amazing, sweetie. We're like that,
we women. All it takes is the right man and…Samantha?
Sam, what is it?''

Sam pulled her hands free of her mother's. "But he
wasn't the right man. Don't you see? I left him because he's
not for me.''

"He was, though, or you wouldn't have become involved
in the first place.''

"Mom.'' Sam gave a little laugh. "I became involved
because he's incredibly sexy. He's one of those men who—
who just steal your breath away.'' She knotted her hands
together. "He wanted me. I wanted him. It was basic stuff.
But he's not the kind of man who'd ever settle down with
one woman.''

"Really,'' Marta said, while a cold knot formed in her
stomach.

"He's the kind of man a woman wants to go to bed with,
not the kind she'd bring home.''

The cold knot was becoming a fist. "Charming.''

"But he was honest. He—he told me how it would be,
that we had no future, and I—I didn't care.'' Sam got to
her feet. "Sex is just sex,'' she said blithely. "That's what
I've always believed. However long our relationship lasted
would be enough.''

"And now you feel differently?''

Sam spun towards her mother. "Did I say that?'' she
demanded. "Why would I feel differently? It was sex. And
it's over.'' Her voice broke. "And I'm pregnant.''

"Yes. That changes things.''

"It doesn't.''

"Samantha, for goodness' sake, of course it does!''

"He doesn't know. And I'm not going to tell him."

"Oh, Sam. You have to!"

"No, I don't."

"Sam. Darling, this baby is half his."

"This baby is entirely mine," Sam said savagely.

Marta watched the transformation in her daughter's face. Her skin went from pale to pink, her eyes from flat to glittering. All good signs, indications Sam was herself again. Too much so, perhaps. That independent streak didn't make sense in this situation.

"Sam," she said, trying to sound reasonable, "no matter what you think this man said about the—the impermanence of your relationship, it's different now."

"It isn't."

"But it is! This man—dammit, what's his name? I can't see myself calling the father of my daughter's child 'this man' forever."

"You're not going to call him anything because you're not going to meet him." Sam lowered her voice. "His name is Demetrios. Demetrios Karas. And that's to stay between us, Mother. I don't want anyone else to know about him."

"Sweetie, honestly, you can't keep a thing like that a secret. Your sisters will—"

"I'll take care of my sisters."

This was not the time to argue, Marta told herself. "Have you considered the difficulties of raising a child alone?"

"If you're saying I'll need money…"

"Yes. You will. We'll be more than happy to help but knowing you—"

"Knowing me, you figure I'd turn you down. And you're right."

"But you don't have a real job." Marta winced as she said it. This was an old sore point between them. "You can't bounce around the globe if you have a child to raise."

"There are lots of good-paying jobs for translators in New York. I just never wanted one before."

"Then think about the baby. Isn't he or she entitled to a father?"

"Carin, Amanda and I did fine without one."

Marta chose to ignore the tossed gauntlet. "Surely, you'll admit Mr. Karas has the right to know he's fathered a child."

"No!"

"Sam—"

"He doesn't want children. He as much as said so."

Marta struggled to keep her temper under control. This son of a bitch who'd bedded her daughter was a mother's worst nightmare. Put bluntly, he was, as the old saying went, a hit-and-run artist. Jonas was right. Someone needed to have a little talk with the man.

"I see," she said calmly. "He's not interested in commitment. He's not interested in children. But he's going to have a child, whether intended or not. And he's obligated to face up to his responsibilities."

Sam's color deepened but her gaze didn't waver. "It's my responsibility, not his. He asked me about protection. I told him I was on the pill. And—and I slipped up."

"So what? Does that mean he gets a free pass? Two people made this baby, Samantha, not one." Marta made a desperate grab at the last of her composure. "Look, honey, lots of men think they don't want children until they actually find themselves having them. Isn't it possible that he has paternal feelings he's never acknowledged? That he might change his mind if he knew you were pregnant? I'm not talking about his marrying you, Sam. From what you tell me of him, you surely wouldn't want him for a husband."

"His parents separated when he was little."

"So what?" Marta folded her arms. "Don't tell me you were taken in by some Casanova's tale of childhood angst!"

"His mother went to live in New York."

"Yes, well, if the gentleman's father was anything like him, I don't blame the lady."

"His father kept custody of their son. Of Demetrios."

"Well, if that was the arrangement—"

"There was no arrangement." Sam wrapped her arms around herself. The room was warm, filled with midday Texas sun, but she was chilled to the bone. "There was just what his father wanted. He's Greek. The rules are different. Men still have rights that we don't even begin to understand. Wealthy, powerful ones, anyway."

"And you think that would happen if...? But you just said, Demetrios Karas doesn't want children."

"And *you* just said that things change, when a man knows he's fathered a baby." She waited, let the seconds slip by until she was sure she could go on. "His father permitted his mother to spend two weeks a year with Demetrios."

"Two weeks?" Marta shook her head. "No. I mean, things aren't like that now. Besides, this is the United States, Samantha. There are laws—"

"Two weeks," Sam said, her voice rising, "in Athens, where the visits could be supervised. And don't waste your breath telling me about laws because if there's one thing the last few months have taught me, it's that men like Demetrios Karas make their own laws." She bit her lip, swung away and stared blindly out the window. "He is never to know about this baby."

"But Sam—"

"Never," Sam said sharply. She turned around. "Promise me, Mom. Swear it."

Marta looked at her daughter. There was more to this. The story about his father forcing his mother to give up her child was disturbing but it left lots of questions unanswered. Talk about wealth and power were all very good—married to Jonas Baron, Marta knew a bit about the iron will of men like that. But a strong woman could face down a strong man, and Sam surely knew she'd have the support of the entire extended Baron clan in a legal fight.

No. There was more, and as she surreptitiously examined her daughter's face, she suddenly knew what it was. Sam had fallen in love. In love with a man who'd made it clear he'd never love her, who'd broken her heart.

"Don't tell Carin and Amanda."

"Oh, Sam!"

"Not yet, okay? Just—just give me time to make some plans."

Marta sighed. "All right."

"And give me your word you'll never let Demetrios know he's fathered my baby."

Marta took her little girl in her arms. "He doesn't deserve to know," she said grimly, and consoled herself by imagining what she'd do to the man if ever she got her hands on him.

A little more than twenty-four hours later, the al Rashids and the Alvareses descended on Espada, their arrivals so closely aligned that the dust of the first Jeep racing in from the ranch's private landing strip barely concealed the rising plume of the second.

Marta kissed her daughters, hugged her sons-in-law and told herself not to have such a suspicious mind. Then she herded them onto the lower level of the waterfall deck, waited until Carmen brought out lemonade and her children had settled into seats before she got down to business.

"Well." She looked around, one brow arched in question. "It's lovely to see you, but I'm too old to believe all of you just happened to pick today to pay a surprise visit."

Silence. Then Rafe cleared his throat. "How is Samantha?"

"She's fine, thank you for ask…" Marta stared at her son-in-law. "How did you know she was here?"

"Well," Amanda said, "she's not in Greece. At least, she's not answering her e-mails. So I tried phoning Demetrios, but I could only reach his housekeeper, and she—"

"She doesn't speak English," Nick said, taking his wife's hand. "Amanda told me she was worried about Sam, so I tried reaching Demetrios at his office. His secretary said he'd gone without leaving a forwarding number, which was strange. He's never out of touch with his office.''

"Never," Rafe said.

"His secretary didn't know anything about Sam, so—"

"So," said Carin, clearing her throat, "I began calling her apartment in New York, leaving messages on her answering machine, but she didn't pick them up." She smiled at her husband. "I told Rafe that Amanda and I were going crazy—"

"And," Rafe said, with deceptive carelessness, "I tried this and that and the other thing and finally I spoke to somebody who knew somebody at the Athens airport, and they did some checking..."

"And we learned that Samantha left Athens and flew to Austin a few days ago," Nick said. "So, here we are."

Marta stared from one innocent face to the other. "Here you are," she finally said. "Just like that."

"There's nothing wrong with us being here." Amanda's tone oozed defense. "We love her. And if something happened that upset her..."

"Why would you even think that?" Marta narrowed her gaze on her daughter.

"Well, she left Athens in a hurry," Carin said carefully. "She hasn't called us. And she came here, instead of going home. No offense, Mother—"

"None taken," said Marta, in a voice that would have turned water to ice.

"But we all know Sam. She'd sooner eat nails than admit she needed help."

"Why would she need help?"

"Mother," Amanda said, "for heaven's sake, must you keep asking 'why'? All we're saying is that Sam's behavior is, well, weird. We love her. We decided to come see if she's okay."

"The four of you flew to Espada, rather than make a simple phone call to the ranch?"

Carin and Amanda exchanged looks. "Well," Carin said, "well—"

"Oh, let's stop beating around the bush," Amanda said. "Look, we, uh, we sort of...we kind of... We thought Sam and this man—"

"Demetrios Karas," Marta said coolly.

"Yes. We thought they might hit it off. So we, um, we tried to introduce them. And then Demetrios told Nick he needed a translator, and I mentioned it to Sam, and—"

"Your sister and Mr. Karas hit if off, all right." Marta glared at her girls.

"Oh." Amanda looked at Carin. "We, uh, we weren't sure how well they—"

"A poor choice of words," Marta said. "Because it isn't well at all. Samantha is pregnant. And your Demetrios Karas doesn't want any part of her."

Amanda and Carin looked thunderstruck. Rafe and Nick surged to their feet, their expressions the same as Jonas's had been the prior day.

"Is that right?" Rafe growled.

"Doesn't he?" Nick snarled.

"Dammit," Sam said furiously, from the lawn below the deck. "Mother, you promised!"

Everyone rushed to the railing. "Darling," Marta said, "I swear, I didn't tell them you were here."

"Sam?" Amanda stared at her sister. "Oh, Sam," she whispered, "I'm so sorry. I never meant—"

"Why didn't you want Mother to tell us?" Carin said. "We love you, Sam. We want to help you."

"I've had enough help from you. All of you." Sam raised her flushed face and glared at her family. "People shouldn't meddle in other people's lives."

"Well, we're going to meddle in Karas's life," Nick said, his voice taut with fury. "When I find that son of a bitch—"

"When *we* find him," Rafe said sharply.

"When we find Karas, he's going to wish he'd never been born."

The deck door banged open. "Try it," a hard male voice said. "I hope to hell you do."

Demetrios stood in the doorway, face white with rage, eyes hot with it, his fists bunched at his sides.

"Karas," Nick said, his voice cold. He stepped forward. So did Rafe. "I didn't think you'd be stupid enough to show up here."

"Come on." Demetrios took a wider stance and beckoned the men towards him. "Come on, take a swing. I'd love to take you on, the both of you." His voice roughened. "Who in hell are you, any of you, to play God with a man's life?"

"What are you doing here?" Rafe demanded.

"It's none of your business."

"It damn well is," Nick growled. "Answer the question. What are you doing here?"

"I came to talk to Samantha."

"Yeah, well, if you know what's good for you—"

"If I did," Demetrios said gruffly, "I sure as hell wouldn't..." He hesitated. Some of his belligerence seemed to ease. "Is she here?"

Nobody answered, but they didn't have to. Five faces turned towards the lawn. Demetrios moved towards the steps that led down from the deck. Rafe and Nick moved, too, and blocked his way, but he'd already seen her, his Sam, staring up at him as if he were a ghost, and he wondered how she could do this to him, make him want to love her and hate her in the same heartbeat.

She was going to run. He could see it in her posture, run the way she had the night she'd left him, the way she had when they'd first met, but he wasn't going to let her get away with it. She had to face him and tell him why she didn't want him. He'd tell her the same thing. And then— and then—

He took a steadying breath and looked at the two men standing in front of him.

"Get out of my way," he said softly.

Rafe folded his arms. So did Nick.

"This is between Samantha and me, nobody else." A muscle knotted in his jaw. "If I have to go through you, I will. I'll do whatever it takes to reach Sam. Is that clear?"

Marta moved quickly, placed herself between her sons-in-law and Demetrios. She took a long look at the man she'd been prepared to despise. He probably hadn't shaved in a couple of days and his hair looked as if he'd spent hours running his hands through it. But he was, just as her daughter had said, sexy and gorgeous—and he was looking past all of them, looking at her little girl in a way that would surely make any woman's heartbeat quicken.

Sam was looking back at him, her eyes brimming with tears, the only kind of tears a woman should ever cry, Marta thought, and felt her heart lift.

"Of course it's clear," she said softly. "It's as clear as glass. Rafe? Nicholas? Let him pass."

"Marta. You don't mean that. This man—"

"I do mean it. Let him pass." Briskly, she clapped her hands. "Everyone inside." Her daughters frowned. Their husbands looked at her as if she'd lost her mind. "Trust me. Samantha's going to be fine."

She shooed them all through the door, knowing they didn't believe her, that her daughters would argue with her while her sons-in-law paced the house like attack dogs just waiting for a sign that they were needed.

Marta smiled to herself. Men were so predictable. How come she'd forgotten that?

CHAPTER TWELVE

SAM watched in disbelief as her sisters and her tough-as-nails brothers-in-law went into the house.

"We want to help you," Carin had said. Amanda had blinked back tears. And when Demetrios appeared, Rafe and Nick made it sound as if they'd never let him get anywhere near her.

Instead, they'd disappeared. Even her mother had walked away.

Wonderful. The very people who'd all but pushed her into Demetrios Karas's arms had abandoned her. She hadn't been able to hear what they were saying up on the deck, but everyone's body language had been simple enough to read. Her mother was upset, her sisters were frantic, their husbands were infuriated...and Demetrios had gotten his way. It would have been hard to believe if she hadn't seen what he was like when he wanted something.

When it came to displays of bad temper and arrogant, pigheaded stubbornness, he'd always be the winner.

Now he was coming down the wide wooden steps, taking his time, looking macho and irate.

"Sam," he said.

His voice was soft, a whisper of smoke in contrast to the banked anger in his eyes.

"Don't run, Sam. I'm warning you. I have no intention of letting you get away this time."

Don't run? Was that a new command, a variation on "stay"? Sam lifted her chin. He was right, she'd been going to run, though not for whatever reasons his self-conceit would probably dredge up but the choice was hers, not his.

She folded her arms, watched as he came down the last

step and started towards her. She'd been stunned to see him but now that the shock was over, she was sure she knew the reason he'd come after her. Women didn't slip out of Demetrios Karas's bed and steal away in the middle of the night. Maybe it was a good thing he was here. She *hadn't* stolen away; she'd simply left him. There was a difference, and he needed to know it...

But he didn't need to know she was pregnant. He *mustn't* know she was pregnant! Sam felt a stab of panic. In the surprise of the last minutes, she'd forgotten all about that. There were changes in her body, ones she'd finally let herself see—see and love, because her baby had gone from being a nonentity to a new life she longed for.

He stopped a few feet from her and folded his arms. Sam dragged in a breath. Would her baby look like its father? Would it have his eyes? His dark hair? Would looking at her child always remind her of how deeply she'd loved Demetrios?

It was stupid to think about that now. Besides, it wasn't true. She'd only imagined she loved him. What woman in her right mind would love a man like him? All she had to do was look at that infamous scowl to know that there was nothing the least bit lovable about him.

And even though she felt as if his eyes were burning holes in her, he'd never see that she was pregnant. She was wearing an enormous old T-shirt, a relic of her university days, that hung as shapeless as a tent to her knees. Nobody who looked at her could possibly—

"Thee mou," Demetrios whispered. "You are with child!"

Sam didn't hesitate. She turned and ran. He was right behind her.

"Sam? Sam, stop!"

She ran harder.

"Sam!" She could hear the whiplash of anger in the way he called out her name. "Samantha, are you crazy? You are pregnant. Pregnant women should not run."

She raced through the garden, towards the fountain that stood at its hidden heart.

"Are you deaf?" he roared, right on her heels. "I am ordering you to stop!"

That's it, she thought, that was absolutely, positively it. She spun towards him, her blood hot with fury and frustration.

"Sam," he said, and she did what she had so often longed to do, raised her hand and slapped his face.

"Damn you, Demetrios," she said...except, to her horror, she didn't say it. She sobbed it. She was weeping, tears spilling from her eyes like rain from the skies that day, all those months ago, when she'd been stupid enough to let him drag her into his life.

"Kitten," he whispered, and then she was in his arms and he was kissing her.

"Go away." She put her arms around his neck and clung to him. "Go back to Greece," she sobbed between kisses. "Get out of my life."

"I cannot do that, *gataki*." He cupped her face in his hands. He was smiling, she saw, but his eyes were almost as wet as hers. "I *am* your life, just as you are mine."

"You see?" Sam pressed a kiss to his mouth. "You always think you know what I'm thinking. And you don't. How could you possibly know how much—how much—"

"I love you," he said softly. "That is how I know. I adore you, kitten. *Se latrévo.* I love you more than words can ever say." He drew back, just enough so he could lay his hand gently over her belly. "And I will love this child with all my heart, and all the children you and I will have together."

Sam gave a broken little laugh. "There you go, planning my life for me."

"No," he said gruffly, "never that."

"Demetrios." She reached up and clasped his wrists. "I was teasing you."

"And I am serious, sweetheart. I will never make you

feel as if your life is mine to control.'' He took a deep breath, then expelled it. ''My father created a gilded cage for my mother but it was a cage, nevertheless. I will not do that to you. I have a home in New York, Sam. Whenever you wish, we will fly there. If you want to work, you will do so. I love you. I need you. But I do not wish to own you. Do you see?''

''Yes,'' she said, ''oh yes, my love, I do. I see that you are my heart, my soul, my life.''

Demetrios gathered her close and kissed her again. Sam sighed and leaned back in his arms.

''I didn't know about the baby when I left you,'' she said softly. ''Although, to be honest, it wouldn't have changed anything. I'd have gone anyway. I couldn't have stayed, not when I thought you wanted to end things between us.''

''I was such a fool, *kalóz mou*. I should have told you that I loved you. Instead, I hurt us both by trying to convince myself that I didn't.''

''Samantha?'' a man shouted. ''Where are you?''

Sam groaned. ''It's Nick.''

''Sam,'' another man yelled. ''Answer us. Where are you? Are you all right?''

''And that's Rafe.'' Sam smiled at Demetrios. ''They probably figured we've murdered each other by now.''

''Sam?'' a third voice joined in. ''Damnation, girl, you let us know if you're all right, you hear?''

''Oh, hell. Jonas, too.'' She sighed as Demetrios leaned his forehead against hers. ''They're going to find us in a couple of minutes.''

''That's good.'' Demetrios cleared his throat. ''I wish to speak with Jonas. And with Marta.''

Sam looked up at him in surprise. ''Why?''

''I am Greek,'' he said, as if that explained everything.

Her eyebrows lifted. ''What a surprise,'' she said sweetly.

''I am Greek and old world, as you once pointed out. And I wish to ask your mother and stepfather for your hand in marriage.''

"Well," she said softly, eyes bright with love, "in that case, I think you might keep in mind that I am American and new world, and you'd better ask me first."

He knew she was teasing him, that she had already given her answer with her kisses and her tears, but he wanted this moment to be one they would remember all their lives, how they'd admitted what was in their hearts in a garden filled with flowers while water spilled like soft rain from a fountain and filled the air with its music.

Demetrios dropped to one knee and clasped Sam's hand.

"Samantha. I love you more than life itself. I'll be the best husband I can be, if you will marry me and share my life."

Tears welled in Sam's eyes and slipped down her cheeks. "Yes. Oh, yes, Demetrios. I will."

He rose just as footsteps pounded down the path. Jonas Baron burst into the clearing with his wife, his stepdaughters and their husbands on his heels.

"There you are," he yelled, "you lily-livered, no-account, no-good Greek son of a—"

"Son-in-law," Marta said, putting her hand on her husband's arm. "Isn't that what you were going to say, Jonas?"

Jonas looked at the man who stood with his arm around Sam's waist. He was big and hard-looking. And smitten, Jonas thought with delight. Absolutely, totally smitten.

"We have met before," Demetrios said. He stepped forward and cleared his throat. "Perhaps you recall…"

Smitten and nervous, too. Jonas almost cackled with delight.

"Mr. Baron. Jonas. I ask for the hand of your stepdaughter. I love her with all my heart, and she loves me. We very much want your blessing. And yours, of course," he said, flashing a smile at Marta, but steely determination replaced the smile in an instant. "But I should tell you both that if you refuse me the right to marry Sam, I'm going to marry her anyway."

Marta laughed. Jonas grinned, put his arm around his wife's shoulders and held out his hand to Demetrios.

"Son," he said, "welcome to the family."

The four Baron brothers had been tossed out of the house by their stepmother.

"Out, all of you," Marta had said. "You're just in the way here. Go on, take a walk or something until it's time for the ceremony."

Travis, Slade, Gage and Tyler had shot each other looks and made a quick break for the door. It wasn't often a man got away from all the hubbub that went with what their wives insisted on calling a simple little home wedding at Espada.

On the way through the kitchen, they stopped just long enough to grab a couple of six-packs...and to collect three other lost-looking males. Their cousin, Gray, looked as if he was trying to fade into the wall along with Nick and Rafe.

"What are you guys doing in here?" Tyler said in surprise.

"Trying to keep from being caught in the stampede," Rafe muttered.

"Trying to avoid your old man," Gray said bluntly. "I don't think Jonas and I have said more than hello and good-bye in the last ten years but every time I turned around today, there he was."

Slade grinned. "He wants something from you. That's the old here-I-am and by god, there-you-are routine he's so good at."

"Well, that's the problem. 'You want to talk to me, Jonas?' I finally said. And he got this look on his face as if I were crazy. 'What the hell makes you think so?' he said, and wandered away."

"So? Problem solved."

"Yeah." Gray sighed. "Except, he looks like a man with

something on his mind…'' He shook his head and reached for a six-pack. ''How about we get out of here for a while?''

Tyler clapped his cousin on the back. ''The man's a genius,'' he said. ''Is it any wonder he's a big-shot New York lawyer?''

The little group laughed, went out the back door, almost ran over a pair of gardeners giving a last-minute manicure to some shrubs and made a beeline for the barn.

''We used to hold meetings here, when we were kids,'' Travis said. ''Well, Slade and Gage and I did. Nobody ever found us.'' He looked from one man to the other. They were all wearing tuxes, white shirts with ruffles and the pained expressions of men who knew they looked foolish and couldn't do a damn thing about it. ''Anybody worried about gettin' dirt on these monkey suits?'' He waited, then chuckled. ''I didn't think so.''

Moments later, the men of the Baron clan were sitting in the old hayloft, their backs against the planked walls as they soothed their parched throats with gulps of cold beer.

''Man,'' Slade said, ''you'd think women would get tired of these things.''

''Weddings?'' Gage sighed. ''Never.''

''He's right,'' Travis added. ''Women love all this stuff. The flowers. The candles. The music. The fuss. And I'll be damned if I can understand the reason.''

''The reason,'' Tyler said smugly, ''is because they're women.'' His brothers looked at him. So did Nick, Rafe and Gray. ''Well, it's the truth. There are X chromosomes, and Y chromosomes, and—''

''And you can tell the ones that are X's,'' Gray offered, ''because they're dressed in pink.''

''Definitely dressed in pink.'' Nick said solemnly. ''Yeah, I read about that new scientific discovery.''

They laughed, sighed, drank more beer. Rafe cleared his throat.

''The man's okay, you know.''

They all knew what he meant and they all nodded.

"He'd better be," Slade said, after a minute. "Otherwise, we'll set him straight."

"You mean, Sam'll set him straight," Gage said.

The men chuckled.

"She's one tough piece of work," Tyler said, and smiled. "Like my Caitlin."

"Like all of them," Travis said. "Baron men don't marry weak women."

"And Brewster women don't marry weak men."

They mulled that over, looked at Gray who raised his hands as if to say they could count him out. Everybody laughed again, and then Nick raised his beer bottle in salute.

"Here's to Demetrios. All he needed was a good woman to straighten him out."

Bottle clinked gently against bottle. "Yeah," Slade said lazily, "well, some men are like that, I guess."

Nobody made eye contact. Then someone snickered. Seconds later, they were all laughing. They went on laughing until they heard Caitlin calling from below.

"Club meeting's over," she yelled. "Come on down."

"You wanna come up?" Travis yelled back. "There's some beer left, and you're an honorary Los Lobos member."

"Yeah, yeah, yeah. Too little, too late." But her voice had a smile in it that made the men smile, too. "Actually, I'd love to, but they're about to start." She stepped back as the men came down the ladder. "Ushers? Best man? Places, gentlemen. It's time."

It was time, Demetrios thought as he waited at the altar, time for his new life to start.

He and Sam had talked about eloping, just flying to Las Vegas and getting married, but Marta wanted to make her last unmarried daughter a wedding, a real one, she said. Finally Sam said well, maybe a wedding with flowers and music and things—maybe that would be nice. Didn't Demetrios think it would?

What he'd thought was that he'd have walked through fire, if it made her happy, so he'd smiled and said yes, sure, the idea of putting on a silly suit and sharing the most wonderful moment of his life with a bunch of strangers was a great idea. Well, of course, he hadn't said any of that except for the "yes" part…

"Here she comes," Nick said softly.

Demetrios looked up and felt his heart turn over.

Sam, his beautiful Sam, was floating towards him on her stepfather's arm, an exquisite vision in white lace. Her hair was gathered high on her head in a loose knot ringed with tiny white and yellow roses. Her gown had a low neckline and tiny sleeves he'd heard her sisters refer to as caps before Marta had noticed he was in the room and shushed them to silence. The skirt was long and slender, and his gaze lingered on the beautiful little rounding of her belly, where his child lay in unborn slumber.

Jonas brought her to the altar, kissed her cheek and went to sit down beside Marta in the first row of white chairs that had been arranged in the garden.

"Hello," she said softly, smiling up at Demetrios.

He smiled back. "Hello, sweetheart," he whispered and though he knew he wasn't supposed to do it, he bent his head and brushed his bride's soft mouth with his.

"I love you, *gataki*," he murmured. "With all of my heart. And I will love you forever."

Tears of joy glittered in Samantha's eyes. "Forever," she whispered.

Moments later, they were husband and wife.

The world's bestselling romance series.

HARLEQUIN® *Presents*

Seduction and Passion Guaranteed!

Proud, passionate, primal—
Dare she surrender to the sheikh?

Find rapture in the sands in
Harlequin Presents

Surrender To The Sheikh

Coming soon:

THE SHEIKH'S WIFE

by *Jane Porter*

Harlequin Presents #2252
Available in May

Pick up a Harlequin Presents® novel and you will
enter a world of spine-tingling passion and
provocative, tantalizing romance!

Available wherever Harlequin books are sold.

HARLEQUIN®
Makes any time special ®

Visit us at www.eHarlequin.com

HPSTTS

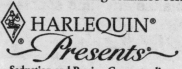

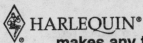

Back by popular request...
those amazing Buckhorn Brothers!

*Once
and Again*

Containing two full-length novels by
the Queen of Sizzle,

USA Today bestselling author

LORI
FOSTER

They're all gorgeous, all sexy and all single...at least for now!
This special volume brings you the sassy and seductive
stories of Sawyer and Morgan Buckhorn—offering you
hours of *hot, hot* reading!

Available in May 2002 wherever books are sold.

And in July 2002 look for FOREVER AND ALWAYS,
containing the stories of Gabe and Jordan Buckhorn!

HARLEQUIN®
Makes any time special ®